GENESIS

J.M. MADDEN

ACKNOWLEDGMENTS

I have to acknowledge my buddy Donna McDonald first. I don't even remember what exactly we were talking about in 'our' Panera that day, but somehow you told me about this plant that shamans used in the jungle called Ayahuasca. My mind went crazy with possibilities! It's been a long time coming, but thank you for that!

Meg, as always, my own personal Wonder Woman. Excellent work!

Siobhan and Sandie, you ladies are such giving souls. I loved your feedback. This book would not be as good as it is without it. Thank you!

I started writing the Lost and Found series way back in 2010. But I didn't start publishing it until 2012 because I didn't know how people would respond to heroes that weren't perfect.

Publishing the series was the best thing I've ever done. It's brought me more satisfaction than I ever expected, and I know for a fact that it has helped some readers heal from their own real-life issues.

Aiden has been a secondary character in several books, but I always had a plan for him. I knew where he belonged. It just took me a while to get him where he needed to be.

I hope you enjoy Aiden's story.

CHAPTER ONE

I f he could have opened his eyes, he would have but there was something obscuring his vision. He tried to lift his right hand but it was so heavy. Probably because he was laying on his side, curled as tightly as he could to try to conserve body heat. Even in the Brazilian jungle it was possible to be cold and hypothermic, especially if your torturers had thrown you into your cage naked after being soaked in a cesspool for hours. If he'd had more energy Aiden would have tried to do something to conserve his body heat but it was all he could do to stay conscious.

It was up to him to stay healthy, he was told. He had the ability to heal himself of the infection eating its way through him.

He heard noises outside but couldn't see what it was. He didn't know that he would even look if he could. Their 'training regimen' didn't change much. At least it hadn't over the past several weeks. It seemed like the further the program progressed the harder they tried to kill the remaining trainees.

Wulfe's turn was up next. The assholes were consistent,

that way at least. As the trainees had fallen the circle had tightened. It used to be Calhoun, Fox and Fournier between him and Wulfe. The Frenchman, Fournier, had been a Commando Marine, the French version of a Navy SEAL. Supposedly they had one of the most difficult training regiments in the NATO Special Forces. It was ironic he had died first because he was supposed to have been the example to follow.

He'd died from an overdose of the Ayahuasca serum, given to him by the technicians on Dr. Shu's orders.

If Aiden could have laughed when it happened, he would have. The fucking idiots had killed their ideal soldier.

Calhoun, the Canadian, hadn't lasted much longer than Fournier; they died within days of each other. Aiden wasn't sure when Fox died, he'd just been out of the rotation one day. A few days later a body bag had been evacced out of the bush by helicopter. That was one of the conditions the countries participating in the study had insisted on. If their 'delegates' were compromised, they were given the body after the post-mortem so that they could take their own samples. Aiden wondered how much was actually left over by the time the powers that be were done chopping the men up. It was sickening what they did to them. All of the men in the camp had earned their place here by serving their individual countries to the best of their ability. They were the elite of the elite. And they were being killed off like dogs in the pound.

Wulfe would be gone for a few hours or so, then taken back to his cage to recover and be monitored. There would be another seven guys to cycle through before it would be Aiden's turn again. So, about a week and a half to recover from yesterday's training.

God, did he even have it in him to keep going?

He'd been here almost four months now. Damn. It had been spring when he'd left California, traveling to Washington for a meeting with representatives of a dozen other special forces groups. There had been Navy SEALs like himself, Airborne, Green Berets and an international assortment of other badasses. It had been an impressive display of talent. Too bad half of them were dead now.

———

The week slogged on. He was completely out of it for a couple of days. He remembered blinking his eyes open to see Wulfe being dragged back to his cage. He hung limp between two guards who struggled to manage the German's bulky frame, his feet leaving lines in the dirt. Normally the sight of the big man so compromised would have depressed the fuck out of him, but he just didn't have the energy for it.

The third day after 'treatment', Aiden could tell his body was beginning to rally. When he sat up in the corner of his cage the world spun briefly, then steadied.

The camp was quiet this early in the morning. Armed guards did their rounds and chatted, sharing cigarettes behind the officers' shacks. The heat was almost manageable now, but he knew within just a couple of hours it would be sweltering again.

Looking at the front of the cage he saw the oat cake that had been left for his dinner. The insects had eaten a chunk but he brushed them away and took a bite, chewing slowly. Bland as always, but he needed the nutrients in the damn thing. It was supposedly juiced with all kinds of vitamins, like a granola bar on steroids. It just didn't taste as good. Dr. Shu had come up with the recipe, claiming that it had everything a body needed. He reached out and rattled the canteen. There might be a swig or two of water. Maybe he should save it for the heat of the day. It was his fault for not having it at the door within easy reach of the guards so that they could refill it. If the guards had to do any more work than the bare minimum, it didn't get done.

Screw it. He took a couple more small bites of the oat cake then a big swallow of water to wash it down. There was another sip in the bottom for later if he needed it.

At eight o'clock, the guards he called Smoke, for his relentless addiction to cheap tobacco, and Buck for his lack of dental care, 'escorted' Fontana to the training facility. Aiden noticed the Navy SEAL actually seemed almost eager to go. As if he felt Aiden's eyes on him Fontana looked up and gave him a wink, then disappeared into the concrete med center where they conducted the experiments.

For some reason that wink put him on edge. Was Fontana going to do something crazy and suicidal? Or was he just trying to make the best of a terrible situation?

Aiden rested for a little while— he wasn't sure how long— then rallied his energy to get up. He rolled to his knees and used the bars on his left to brace himself as he tried to stand. The floor of the cage was a smooth piece of iron, painted with a texturizing material to keep their feet from slipping in the damp humidity. Thighs quivering more than they had in a long time, he forced himself to straighten. Then, shaking out his limbs, he moved to the pipe set in the floor, his 'bathroom', and did his business. He'd gotten used to the humiliation of living like an animal.

The accommodations for the participants left much to be desired. They were prisoners. Period. At first, they had been housed in the barracks along with the guards, but as the testing became more harsh and detrimental to their health, the men had begun to question the validity of the Spartan Project. When the first participant died, then another, and another within a couple of days, the rest had refused to continue. They'd staged a bit of a rebellion, though they were too ingrained with the military structure to do much beyond refusing to participate. That night, the guards had been quietly moved out and the rest of the men in the barracks had been drugged. Aiden assumed they'd used the ventilation system to deliver some type of airborne sedative. The next morning they'd all woken up in cages, seven feet by ten feet. And the Brazilian Army had moved in to keep control. Apparently, the eggheads in charge didn't believe that their own security personnel were able to maintain order.

That had been a wake-up call for all of them. They had been participants in the Spartan Project, 'delegates' from many countries. Now, according to one of the assistants, they were considered 'antagonistic subjects'. Aiden had been royally pissed, but not really surprised. With the amount of clandestine activity he'd seen in the camp escalating— fences going up and more guards and mercenaries being moved in— he'd had a feeling their freedom, maybe their lives, were about to be forfeit.

When he'd signed up for the study he'd been assured that the facility would be state of the art. And it was, to a certain extent. Aiden had been impressed when they'd first gotten here. The research buildings were equipped with every technological and medical device they could possibly need, in spite of the difficulty of getting it to the middle of the Brazilian jungle. The governments participating in the trial had all contributed a huge amount of seed money, so they had plenty of play dough. It was just too bad none of the dough was actually being spent on the *care* of the men.

And while the doctors working on the project all seemed to be top-notch, the man leading the project, Dr. Edgar Shu, was a Nobel Prize winning doctor. He was world-renowned for his work with pediatric cancer. With the backing of the Silverstone Collaborative, a multi-billion dollar pharmaceutical company, he'd developed immunotherapies for half a dozen lethal diseases, saving thousands, if not tens of thousands, of people. He appeared to the world to be a benevolent, dedicated doctor always striving for optimal health for the world's population. But that population didn't see him when the maniacal light lit his eyes at an unexpected test result, or when he had a new, radical idea for a test for one of his subjects. All of the normal constraints a doctor would work under— FDA or NIH guidelines, organizational rules, Hippocratic Oath, the Geneva Convention— had flown out the window when they'd left the country. Brazil didn't care what he did to his subjects, as long as they were paid their hush money.

If Aiden had to listen to one more of the man's rambling, disjointed explanations on why his work was so important to the world, because they needed soldiers that would be able to survive *anything* when the next war came, he would throw himself on the end of a guard's weapon and ask to be shot. It was irritating in the extreme listening to the man explain away all of their pain and agony with a bucket of bullshit, 'You're helping to guarantee a better life for our world's most important citizens.'

Aiden took that to mean that the Collaborative would not be producing whatever they created for the general population. No, it would be for the few that could afford to purchase it. There was no way the Collaborative was doing this out of the goodness of their hearts. Yes, their company founder Damon Wilkes appeared to be a philanthropist, but they'd had to make money somewhere for the company to be as big as it was. His collaboration with the governments in the Spartan Project hinted at widespread corruption. The government considered the men equipment anyway, no better than shovels, used to get a job done. There was always someone willing to benefit or profit from their use. Or abuse.

Leaning into the far corner of the cage he craned his neck to try to see Wulfe. The big German lay curled on his side, bones poking out of his naked hips. They'd all lost weight but Wulfe seemed leaner than the rest, or maybe he just looked that way because of his size. Focusing his thoughts and energy, he gave a mental shout. *Wulfe!*

Wulfe didn't jerk but his dark head lolled till he blinked up at the ceiling. *Yes.*

Aiden tried not to grin or do anything the cameras mounted in each corner of the cage would catch. *Hey buddy. I was worried about you.*

I also worried. But I think I will be better soon. This sickness was not so bad.

Though they hadn't spoken much when they'd been in the barracks, Aiden could still hear Wulfe's German accent strongly in his mind. *Yes, I agree. Are we getting stronger or was this an easier test?*

He could just barely see Wulfe blink at the question. *Not sure. Maybe both.*

When he'd first heard about the trial, he'd laughed to himself. The thought that a jungle plant could make them extraordinarily strong was pretty outrageous. But if the government was willing to spend money on it they must have something to back up their claims. The only thing shown to the subjects was a single video of an indigenous Amazon shaman running through the treetops. At first nothing had seemed off, then the camera zoomed back and they had the scope of the distances he was leaping, and the size of the trees he climbed. The brown skinned man had seemed like a real life Tarzan on steroids.

But that two minute clip had apparently just been the tip of the iceberg. Dr. Shu had told them of other instances when Ayahuasca users had shown amazing strength and dexterity, as well as off the charts mental growth. The fervid light that shone in his eyes was enough to make Aiden wonder if it was all true.

It had been after a particularly brutal 'test' that Wulfe had gone through when they'd first made the mental connection. They'd known everything they said, every look, was monitored, so Aiden had bitten his tongue and watched as they'd carried the limp form of his friend past.

Aiden had been cursing the government and the doctors in his head, screaming inside his skin, when another voice had penetrated.

Quiet, please, American.

Aiden had reeled back from the bars, wondering what the hell he'd just heard. *What?*

You heard me. You blame government and doctors, but you volunteered, yes? Now we deal with consequences.

Wulfe?

Yes! Now be quiet while I try to fix.

He'd been stunned into silence. Even now, weeks later, he was always surprised when he received a response to his mental call. And even more disbelieving that they could carry on an actual conversation.

Aiden had quieted his mind, though his thoughts had raced. That incident had happened several weeks ago, and they had been talking ever since. As their energy would allow anyway. It was taxing at first, but as they became more competent at it their strength grew, like any other muscle.

Aiden thought the doctors had expected a purely physical response to the serum they were using on the group, and to an extent they received that. The men were able to fight off diseases, but they certainly didn't have the ability to swing through the trees or anything. At least, not that they knew of. The subjects hadn't been let out of their cells for anything other than the walk to the med center since their attempted mutiny in the barracks.

They did not inform the doctors about the stunning mental development, though. The testing would have undoubtedly intensified. He and Wulfe, the only two able to communicate this way so far, would probably have forfeited their lives.

Fontana had been the next they'd heard. One day when they'd been 'escorting' the Navy SEAL back to his cage Aiden had tried to contact him. The man had looked up in surprise, then glanced at the guards on either side of him. When his gaze had connected with Aiden, he'd given him a small nod.

Proximity definitely seemed to play a part in the communication. Wulfe's cage sat only about twenty yards away. Fontana had only been about five yards away as he'd walked back toward his cage. As he was able, Aiden began sending thoughts to the returning men. Some he connected with—others he did not.

Most, he didn't.

But he could see the hope in the men's expressions when they neared his cage. Aiden cautioned them to play it safe and to keep this part of their...*evolution*... a secret. They were all smart men and agreed. But every day that passed their expressions asked what they were going to do to get out of the situation.

The problem was, were they willing to go AWOL? Technically, they were all still part of their respective military units, but the fact that they were being held against their will and the parameters of the exercise had shifted didn't really change anything. If they walked away under their own power, the Collaborative and their hired mercenaries would be after them. Aiden had no doubt that if those behind Spartan feared exposure, they would eliminate the threats.

The men themselves.

If word got out that a shadowy government organization was murdering innocent military test subjects, there would be an international uproar. But even in that best case scenario, their lives would still be forfeit. They would continue to live in a fishbowl, under constant scrutiny to see what effects Shu's testing had on their bodies and minds.

So, they bided their time.

Then one day, something changed.

Aiden and Wulfe were recovering from their most recent trial, an exploration of electrical burns that left them riddled with seeping blisters. In spite of the jungle temperature he was racked with cold chills. It took all of his concentration not to slip into a blissful coma, oblivious to anything going on around him. Some inner sense told him that if he gave into the waiting dark he wouldn't see the light again.

Wulfe? You okay big man?

There was no response.

Given his height and breadth, the doctors believed they could experiment on him more than the others. Fearing the worst for his solitary friend, Aiden gathered his energy to push.

What? Wulfe snapped in his mind.

Just checking on you my friend. And trying to block off my own pain.

Yes. I'm still here.

Even in his mind Aiden could hear the gritty determination in the man's mind. It bolstered his own determination to beat this trial.

Aiden lost himself for a few hours, encouraging his body to heal itself. They hadn't figured out the exact mechanics of the ability, only its results. Though he expended a lot of energy healing himself, the results became clear almost immediately. His cold chills eased and some of the blisters absorbed back into his body. They didn't have enough hydration to spare to splitting blisters.

When the guard came around to fill their water canisters, Aiden hurriedly drank the last swallow before setting the bottle near the door, then moved back to the corner of his cell. God, his skin burned. Already several large patches had sloughed off, leaving raw pink patches behind. Keeping the insects away from the wounds was a futile endeavor but he tried, constantly waving his hands over the worst wounds.

The guard, Smoke, growled at Aiden like he always did, but before he left he dropped a second oat cake into the pan. The bottle was filled completely to the top with water before the cell door clanged shut.

Aiden blinked, wondering what the hell had just happened. Why had he given him two? Crawling forward he looked at the oat cakes and water, then nibbled and drank. They tasted as horrid as they always did. Gritting his teeth he sat and ate one of the cakes, the whole thing, washing it down with hearty gulps of water. For the first time in weeks his belly felt full and satisfied.

Wulfe.

Yeah?

What's up with Smoke? Did you get two?

Yes. Not sure. Taking advantage while I can.

Yeah, me too.

Nothing was said about the extra food that day. Aiden had long suspected that the guards trimmed the prisoner's allotment for their own benefit. Had Smoke suddenly grown a conscience?

Doubtful.

The next day Aiden felt much better, so much so that one of the assistants doing well checks remarked upon it and jotted something in his chart. Aiden wished the little punk would come close enough to the bars to snap his scrawny neck. Colin seemed to sense the danger because he stayed well clear of the cage.

He took the same care at Wulfe's cage but didn't seem as impressed with his progress.

Then it was Fontana's day in the med center. Once again

when he walked by, he gave Aiden a lazy smirk, as if he were the one running the entire operation. Aiden puzzled on the look for a long time and waited for the SEAL to return. When he did, Aiden was stunned. It didn't look like anything had been done to him. There were no bruises or restraint marks. Definitely no burn marks, like he and Wulfe were dealing with. He looked a little ill, but nothing like before. As the man walked by Aiden couldn't help but look into his eyes.

Fontana winked at him. *Did you like the extra oat cake? Smoke is very susceptible to suggestion. Finesse him.*

Shock roared through Aiden's mind and it was all he could do to keep his expression still. What the fuck?

Out of his peripheral vision he watched Fontana walk away, one of the strongest of the group. Was that how he had done it? By coercing other people to do things for him? Aiden wanted to ask the man questions but there was no time. He'd already disappeared beyond Wulfe's cage, beyond Aiden's line of sight.

Wulfe, did he talk to you?

Aiden rolled over deliberately, trying to hide the tension in his body by curling up and hiding his face.

Yes. Crazy, I think.

Is he really though? Why would Smoke have given us extra if he didn't have to?

The silence was prolonged.

Maybe we need to explore this. We have a few days before next trial.

———

Smoke apparently took a day off, because Aiden didn't see him until the following night, and then it was only briefly. The man walked by and tossed in a small folded towel. He started to walk away but Aiden stared at him, focusing his mind on a single question. *What is your name?*

"Hernando", Smoke answered immediately.

Aiden let him go.

Fuck...

CHAPTER TWO

There had been a carefully written note hidden in the folds of the towel. Aiden made sure to glance at the thin paper out of sight of the cameras in the corners of his cell.

Planning a party. Be ready.

Damn. Not much to go on. He crumpled the paper as tight as he could and sent it down the piss tube.

Wulfe.

Yes, American.

I think Fontana has something planned. Not sure when but Smoke just dropped me a note.

Fontana is going to get us all killed with his games.

No, I don't think so. I asked Smoke what his name was mentally, and he answered me out loud. I think Fontana is on to something.

There was silence for several long minutes. *I will try with the other guard.*

Aiden didn't need to tell him to be careful. They were all being as careful as they dared, but they had to get out of this place. He'd started to give in to the despair of being away from home and his regular life for so long. Their bodies had maintained so far, but what if whatever Dr. Shu and his cronies came up with next killed them? The experiments themselves had already escalated. Yes, they were getting better about repairing what damage was done to them, but at some point their torturers would find something they couldn't recover from.

There were ways to get in and out of the camp. When Aiden had first been imprisoned he'd watched every single movement, desperate to memorize everything. The routine hadn't changed much over the months. There were food and personnel deliveries once a week, and a maintenance truck came at least once a week. There was a fuel truck that came twice a week. If they could plan their escape around one of those times it might give them some cover.

How many would be able to travel? Aiden and Wulfe, definitely. Fontana and the young Army Ranger, Rector. The other men had slowly dwindled away. Aiden vowed to himself to stay aware and watch who was still active, and he would try to speak to each prisoner that passed. If they made contact, it would be one more person for their team.

Two unfamiliar Army guards stopped outside his cell. Aiden was confused because it wasn't his testing day. Standing, he prepared to be shackled and led away, but it didn't happen.

"Turn around," the taller guard ordered.

Aiden did as he was told, hating having his naked back to men he didn't know, even just by their faces. The lock on his cage door rattled and he heard the door swing open, then there was some fumbling. It sounded like they were working on his cameras.

"Looks fine," the man murmured in Portuguese. "I don't know what Ortega thought he saw."

They fumbled for a few more minutes and barked something over the radio. They received a response, then left the cage, door slammed shut behind them. They didn't tell him he could stand down, just left him there. Aiden eventually turned his head enough to check their proximity. He looked up at the cameras in the corners but didn't see anything different. If they had messed with them he couldn't tell what they'd done.

Relief edged through him that they hadn't expected anything from him and he sagged down to the floor. Every time they came toward him with the shackles in their hands, his throat would tighten with fear. He hated to admit that even to himself, but it did. They'd programmed him that when they latched on the cuffs, pain was coming. These two today hadn't had cuffs with them, but they'd had the cattle prods and they'd been in uniform, which had been enough to send his fear response racing.

Two days later it was his turn in the rotation for 'training' and he had to fight that choking fear again as he turned to face the wall. Aiden tried to prepare himself for whatever was to come but it was so hard, not knowing what he'd be facing. They'd dealt with every kind of common, contagious sickness known to man, it seemed like; colds, flu, meningitis. But it seemed like they were moving into injuries now, and how they recovered from them. As he walked into the facility, he dragged his dignity around his naked self like armor. They could do whatever they wanted, but they would not break him. He came from a tough life. He was one of only six men out of a hundred that survived his hell week when he'd tried out for the SEALs. This was just another chapter. Aiden shut that corner of his mind off and tried to prepare himself. It would be painful and senseless, but he would damn well live through it.

They would not defeat him. No one had ever given him a hand up in this life. He'd had to fight for every single thing he'd ever had, and he didn't expect this to be any different. There was no one on this property stronger than he was, and he would make it out of this godforsaken jungle alive.

Dr. Shu, a man hired because of his sadistic personality as much as his scientific research, had put them through stress tests at the beginning. How far could they run? How long could they hold their breath without passing out? All baseline information, they were told, in preparation for the real testing.

Once they'd been at the camp a couple of weeks the actual experimentation had started. The first test had been to fight off the common cold, then three different variations of the flu strain. Those everyday illnesses had taken out three men, as much because of the Ayahuasca dosage levels at the sickness itself. The Ayahuasca was originally developed by indigenous shamans for religious rituals, but poultices made from the plant had been shown to slow bleeding. So, the doctors had derived a serum from concentrated Ayahuasca plant suitable for injection and given that to the men before the trauma or illness was 'administered'. In other words, they'd gotten shots before they were contaminated with whatever the flavor of the week was. The plant itself had several different strains and had to be boiled down into a thick syrup, which then had to be diluted in something to be injectable.

When the project had first started, Dr. Shu had been guessing at the amount of derivative it took to administer the proper dosage per kilo of body weight. All of the information he'd had about the Ayahuasca was second hand knowledge and hearsay. After they'd figured out a moderate level that healed the men without killing them, they moved on to bigger and more dangerous things.

Meningitis had knocked him down for a double rotation, but he'd survived it. Typhoid did as well. Several of the men had developed malaria naturally from the mosquitos in the environment around them and recovered without treatment.

Then one night one of the region's poisonous vipers decided to crawl into his cell to taste him. Snake bite was a standard wartime hazard, so the techs and Dr. Shu considered his misfortune a learning experience. For three days Aiden stayed in the med center, his blood being drawn every hour to monitor the progress of the venom. It had been one of the hardest things he'd ever had to survive. For days he'd been out of his mind with fever as his body tried to combat the poison. When he'd finally become coherent enough to know where he was, he could tell he'd lost a large amount of weight. He still had an occasional shimmy in his hands that he thought could be attributed to that incident.

He received his regular weekly shot, and the symptoms of the venom had faded away. They hadn't given it to him early because they wanted to 'stick to the schedule as closely as possible'.

Now they knew that if you were bitten by a highly venomous viper with a fast acting neurotoxin, the Ayahuasca could only slow the spread of the toxin. And it wouldn't help with the residual effects. But if you had a slower acting trauma, it had startling recuperative effects. The Ayahuasca would make you better, it just took a while.

So, the doctors had learned to shape their tests accordingly. They were working their way through poisons and illnesses, one per week, one each per testing group.

When he was shoved into the building, he was immediately escorted to the shower room. It was the only time they got clean, right before testing. There was no scrubbing, just a torrent of lukewarm water from a faucet overhead and a brick of yellow soap. It was bliss. The only enjoyment he got in this damn place. Aiden tried to prolong it as much as he could, because it felt really good to get all of the accumulated sludge off of his body. He scrubbed at the stubble on his head. The handcuffs made it difficult to reach everywhere though, and they were a constant reminder of where he was.

They never went anywhere without the sexy bracelets. There had been a few incidents when the guards had been overwhelmed by the captives. That was when the Army had moved in and had begun doing the transports. And they had batons and cattle prods if the subjects forgot their places again.

Once he was fairly clean he was positioned in front of a fan to dry, then escorted to the testing hallway. People in lab coats walked the over lit corridors, barely glancing at his naked form because so many had come through there. Aiden actually tried to make eye contact with a few people, but they had been trained to avoid even the slightest hint of impropriety. It infuriated him to be dismissed so casually.

When they entered the testing room, Aiden did his best not to struggle, but he knew the pain was coming. He didn't know what form it would take, but he knew it would be devastating.

In desperation he looked at the lab tech moving in to secure his wrists to the bed shackles.

Please, don't do this.

The man's hands fumbled. Not daring to hope, Aiden stared at him as hard as he could. *Don't put those shackles on me. Something is wrong with them.*

The tech turned the shackles in his hands, looking at the leather. He moved the posts that slid through the holes and flipped it over. He glanced at Aiden. "These look fine," he said, and moved back in to fasten the pieces around his wrists.

Aiden didn't want to jeopardize any escape Fontana had planned, so he swallowed down his panic and allowed the man to secure him to the tilt table. He closed his eyes, refusing to acknowledge whatever was coming.

In a moment they'd lay him horizontal and inject him with their experiment of the week. He waited, breath held, as one of the vacant-gazed medical techs moved in and applied sensors across his body, then two at his temples. She strapped a blood-pressure cuff to his arm, and an oxygen sensor to his finger. Then she left the room the same way she'd entered. She didn't lay the table down.

Aiden panted, the anticipation making his heart rate pick up on the beeping monitor. Eventually someone would come in with a needle and he'd fight the restraints just like he always did, though he knew it wouldn't matter. In the end they were stronger than he was. At least for now.

They left him alone long enough that he actually started to relax. He should've known better. He closed his eyes to block out the blinding light from the overhead fluorescents.

Only then did he hear a slight thumping noise.

Aiden opened his eyes when a sharp crack of sound ricocheted through the small space. Blinding, excruciating pain ripped through his lower left side. He gasped and tried to curl into it, but he couldn't move because of the straps. For a moment it just felt like he'd had the air knocked out of him, then it began to focus. Oh, fuck, it *hurt*. Nausea swirled through his gut and he forced himself to look down. A bullet had ripped through his side. The entry wound wasn't large, but he could feel the exit wound on his back. Blood flowed down his side and when he shifted his feet, the left one squelched in blood. He looked down at the curtain of red sweeping down his thigh, so stark against his skin. This was going to be bad.

No one moved to help him. The tech who'd fastened him in had a blatant grin on his mouth, just for Aiden to see. It pissed him off that they had been reduced to disposable animals for the enjoyment of these sickos.

He glanced up to the two-way mirror across from him. It had slid over about two feet, something he hadn't been aware it could do, and the muzzle of a rifle rested on the sill. The space behind the weapon was completely black, but Aiden could feel the casual disregard and antagonism rolling off the shooter. The man's hands felt tied, as surely as Aiden's. He was a sharpshooter for the Army and he wanted to kill, but Capitão Aguirre wouldn't let him. Aiden could feel the enjoyment the man took in shooting people, and how unsatisfying the single shot to merely wound was to him. The task had been too easy. He wanted to shoot again.

Aiden felt the man's emotions as clearly as if they were his own. Through the blazing pain, he looked at the smirking tech. Trying to concentrate in spite of the pain, he turned the shooter's attention there, to the piece of shit who'd brought him there and fastened him into these cuffs.

And just that easily the man was dead, a perfect bullet hole through his smirking face.

Aiden knew he should feel bad about taking advantage of the shooter's feelings and motivations, but he didn't. Not after what they'd just done to him.

Confusion exploded. People screamed and guards came from nowhere, shouting at the shooter to lay down his weapon. A light flipped on in the room next door and Aiden could see the dark-haired native man. He seemed sincerely confused as he looked at what he had done, then at Aiden, fastened securely to the table and still bleeding. There was no explanation for what had happened.

The guards marched the sniper from the building and Aiden heard shots fired outside. Without opening his eyes, he knew the sniper was gone. Fuck you, bastard.

He watched orderlies remove the tech's body through

slitted eyes. They refused to look at him. He was still a test subject, and in spite of what had gone on around him they would still monitor his test. Lousy motherfuckers.

Time stilled. While his body worked to repair the damage, he sank into himself. Aiden could imagine his sidearm in his hands. He pressed the button and released the mag, setting it aside, then he released the slide and the spring. He took the Mk. 25 apart in his mind, rebuilt it, then repeated the process... over and over again to take his mind off the pain. When he was calmer, he allowed his body to relax.

He wanted to test Smoke again. The hesitation on the tech's part had been enlightening, and if there hadn't been so many people in the immediate area, he probably would have tested the man further. The sniper's actions had been the most telling, the most chilling. Aiden knew without being told that this new ability, being able to provoke action on desires, was potentially catastrophic. He wanted to get the hell out of the jungle and back stateside but he honestly wasn't sure what awaited him there. Probably a bullet in the head if he tried to break out of here.

He was vaguely aware of being unfastened from the table and being dragged back to his cell. His mind continued to block out the pain, sapping his energy.

Aiden was aware of days passing, but only through a kind of haze that came over him. His body had slipped into a kind of ... coma, though he heard and felt everything going on around him. He was too exhausted to get to his water or food, but at some point one of the guards slipped in and forced some water down his throat. It felt cool and refreshing, which told him more than anything how fucked up he was. If the tepid water felt cool, that meant he was hot, probably with fever.

He hated this godforsaken jungle.

CHAPTER THREE

American! Willingham! Wake up!

Aiden blinked at the telepathic shout, coming awake with a rush of adrenaline. It only took him seconds to hear the sound of a low flying helicopter. He rolled his head to look through the bars of his cage, but he couldn't really see anything. People were on the move, though. Army soldiers were running to formation in front of the main troop barrack to the east, and some of the doctors were hurrying toward where he knew the helicopter pad was. Actually, it was no more than a spot cut into the foliage just large enough for the blades. It had to be constantly maintained or the jungle would reabsorb the space.

Who is it? Do you know?

No.

Wulfe sat watching the goings on, but Aiden didn't think he could do that. Craning his head he looked down at his gut. The entry wound had scabbed over. There was a little swelling, but nothing too bad, and miraculously, it didn't seem to be infected. Actually, he didn't feel too bad. Using his arms against the bars he pulled himself up, then leaned against the corner. Nausea threatened when he moved and the muscles in his stomach quivered, but they held.

The sound of the helicopter's engines whined as it changed elevation. A sleek, dark Sikorsky flashed through the trees before it disappeared behind the foliage. Aiden didn't have the energy to wonder who it was coming to look at them. Probably another nondescript official from one of the countries, or maybe one of the Silverstone executives, checking the 'fiscal viability of the endeavor'. They came every few weeks, looking well-fed and useless, swatting at mosquitos like it would do any good.

There was no sound for a while and his eyes drifted shut, then suddenly there was a flourish of noise and activity. Guards stood at his cell door, waving their weapons at him to get up. Aiden scowled and shook his head, trying to appear more injured than he actually was, but they persisted. Finally, Aiden rolled over onto his knees and dragged himself vertical by using the bars of the cage. The scab around his wound pulled but didn't rip. Breathing deeply, he turned to face his audience.

Expecting another group of men in business suits, he was startled to see a sleekly styled brunette with bright blue, intelligent eyes. The dark navy suit she wore seemed so incongruous in the middle of the jungle, but she didn't even seem to be aware of the surroundings. A waft of expensive perfume hit him, reeking of elegance, but the expression on her face was chilling. She looked at him like he was a piece of meat.

"I really hope you have more to show me than a starving man with a bullet hole in his side."

Aiden scowled, not appreciating the description. As he looked down at himself though, he could see she spoke the truth. He was on the scrawny side.

Dr. Shu adjusted his thick glasses and stepped forward, clipboard in hand.

"But madam, he's standing. The subject was shot less than twelve hours ago, and the skin is completely sealed over."

Aiden blinked, shock rolling though him. He'd thought days had passed since he'd been shot. Letting his head roll forward, he looked at the long line of his stomach again. It had only been twelve hours?

His fingers reached down to touch the wound. It was tender, but not excruciating like it should have been.

What the fuck...

The woman cocked her hip and crossed her arms beneath her breasts. "How long has he been here?"

"Seven months, Madam. Almost eight."

That was another shock. Damn, had it really been so long?

With a disdainful look, she turned away, heading down the row. Four heavily-built men dressed in black combat armor, obviously mercenaries, followed her. The doctor trotted along behind, shuffling file folders as she stopped at each cage.

When she stopped at Wulfe's cage, something about her demeanor changed. Suddenly she seemed more ... predatory. Like if Wulfe was chained to a table she would reverse cowboy him. Nausea surged through Aiden at her avid, sensual interest.

Aiden slid down the bars till his ass hit the ground and rested his head back against the cool iron, wondering how the hell they were all going to get out of this situation.

A short while later, two shots were fired. Two bodies were dragged into the med center. Apparently not everyone had survived the inspection.

———

The woman brought chaos with her. The guards and hired soldiers had been policed by a small crew of Brazilian Army, commanded by Captain Aguirre, a self-important dickhead who'd been responsible for several of the men's deaths. When they'd first been contained two men had tried to break away and Aguirre's squad had shot them down. Another test subject was 'put down' when he'd gone off his rocker, believing the plants were creeping into his cell to eat him. To beat them he'd started eating himself, starting with his calf.

No one had had any idea how severe the psychedelic effects of Ayahuasca could be. Shu had asked all of them if the man, a Czech who had belonged to the 601st Special Forces Group, had had any kind of mental illness they'd noticed. No one had offered any information, but personally, Aiden thought the man had been crazy before he'd been brought to the Brazilian jungle. There'd just been a look in his eyes. The Ayahuasca was known for releasing mental inhibitions, obviously both the good and the bad.

So, Aguirre executed the man rather than risk anyone getting hurt. Aiden probably would have done the same thing, but Aguirre had also taken out a couple of men that hadn't deserved to be extinguished. One subject had spit on Aguirre's boot for some slight. The captain had taken out his service weapon and shot the subject, to Shu's outrage. Another subject, not recovering well from the current experiment, hadn't responded to some obscure order thrown at him as they'd moved him from the med center. When the man had tried to speed up he'd been tripped up by the shackles around his ankles, falling into one of the guards. The guard, already twitchy, had fired several rounds into the camp as his finger contracted on the trigger of his weapon. Aguirre had almost been shot. Instead he'd drawn his weapon and killed the subject. Then he'd also killed the guard.

Aguirre believed himself the ruler of all in the camp. Until the Bitch in Blue arrived.

The guards and the techs talked about the woman like she was some kind of goddess— a warrior woman, beautiful and fierce. Aiden memorized every detail he could learn about her. Because at some point, he was going to kill her.

Priscilla Mattingly, the Chief Operations Officer of the Silverstone Collaborative, stayed in the camp for a week, every day wearing a different blue outfit. In spite of the heat and dangerous terrain, she wore long sleeved power suits and heels, always. Perhaps because of her feminine appearance Aguirre thought he could rule her as he did the camp and the other Silverstone Collaborative executives who'd come before. He realized the mistake in his thinking when Mattingly began directing 'his' troops. It was the highpoint of Aiden's stay at the camp because the intersection of the two strong personalities just happened to take place right in front of his cage.

Mattingly had instructed one of Aguirre's troops standing at the door of the med center building to retrieve her shade umbrella, her only concession to the heat, as she inspected the subjects. The man had jumped to do her bidding, obviously aware of the danger hidden beneath the silk. As the soldier took off running, Aguirre had stepped from the med center and called the boy to attention. Torn, the young soldier had halted, giving Mattingly an apologetic look. When Aguirre asked the boy what he was about, the young soldier had explained.

Aguirre had smiled at the boy, pulled out his sidearm and shot him on the spot. "No one gives orders to my troops but me," he'd growled.

Rage surged through Aiden at the man's casual disregard. The young soldier had been between a rock and a hard place.

A coldness had slid into Mattingly's blue eyes and she'd

waved her guard dogs back as she stepped toward Aguirre. The captain straightened and hooked his thumbs into the pockets of the tan uniform pants. Even as sick as he was at that point, Aiden could see the masculine posturing. Whether intentional or not, the captain pointed his fingers at his dick, reminding the little woman that *he* was the boss. It was an age-old move studied by many behaviorists over the generations. And it was obviously a move she'd dealt with before.

Mattingly didn't acknowledge the action, just stepped around the body of the young soldier and into the captain's space. Some of his guards moved behind him, but they didn't seem to be foolhardy enough to try to save the man.

"I think you're a bit confused as to how things operate around here, Captain."

"No, Senhora. But perhaps you are. Would you like to join me in my hut for a conversation?"

Aiden couldn't believe the man's balls.

Priscilla Mattingly's smile spread, as if she'd just been given a gift. "I'm not sure if you're aware, Captain, but we investigated you quite thoroughly before we had the General appoint you. We were aware of your alcohol problem, as well as the money you've been skimming off your guards' pay." The men shifted behind him, anger suffusing their faces. The captain snapped his mouth shut, losing his smug look. "If either of those misdeeds didn't catch up with you, we figured the drug lord you've been taking bribes from would get tired of losing product when you were supposed to reroute patrols. We put you in this position because we knew, at some point, you'd fuck up, and we'd need a fall guy. You are very close to becoming that fall guy. If you don't straighten up, I'm going to strip you down and put you in one of the cages with these men. Or perhaps I'll let some of your men fuck you. I hear they like that type of thing here and I think they'd enjoy that.

Do you understand what I'm telling you? You're not in charge anymore. I am. After I leave, IF I leave, I may let you be in charge again, but until then, if I tell any of your men to do something, hell, if I tell *you* to do something, I expect to be obeyed immediately. Do you understand me, Captain?"

Red had suffused the man's face and he scowled. "You have four men to my thirty. Do you really think you can control us?"

Mattingly leaned forward and scraped a blood-red nail down the man's cheek. "Try me, you illiterate swine," she whispered. Then she slapped him. Not a hard, decent slap, but one of contempt.

The captain reached for his weapon, not used to being disrespected, but the woman had been waiting for him to move. With a rather elegant twist, she drew a slim knife from the sleeve of her suit jacket. With little fanfare, she turned the knife and shoved it up through the captain's jaw, through the soft palate and into his brain, slamming it as deep as it would go. The captain's eyes widened and he fell slowly to the ground.

The men behind him lifted their weapons, but Priscilla Mattingly gave them a disgusted look and the men lowered the muzzles.

"Just for clarity," she said, leaning down to wipe her bloody hand on the captain's shirt and remove her stiletto, "I am in charge, no matter what clothing you wear. My company is bankrolling every single one of you fuckers, so if you have a problem with that, you need to leave now."

No one moved.

It had been a stunning show of cold authority and it had told them the woman would do anything for her company. It also told Aiden that she would deal with the test subjects the same way if they ever crossed her.

Within three days she'd had the camp running on a

regular schedule. She'd appointed a new 'captain' and the man fell over his feet trying to please her. He followed every new rule she handed down to the letter.

Confident that things were running smoothly, she left a week later. The tension in the camp eased, and things settled back into rhythm. Well, until Shu fell to a violent, bloody death at the fangs of a Bushmaster.

Aiden heard the news from Wulfe, who had overheard some of the soldiers talking about what had happened. Apparently, the viper had been in his hut and the doctor had inadvertently stepped on the thing. The snakes were one of the most aggressive in the jungle anyway, so Aiden knew the bite had to have been devastating. Men had responded to the doctor's cries for help, and the snake had been killed, but the medical response had been insufficient. They'd worked on the doctor for two days, but he had succumbed. Scuttlebutt between the guards said it had been a gruesome death, the venom not allowing the doctor's blood to coagulate.

For days everything medical stopped. The other doctors and technicians seemed to be at a loss as to what to do. Dr. Shu had run every aspect of the Spartan Project and was the Silverstone Collaborative's shining star. They had made *billions* off the man and his cures for diseases.

Aiden wondered if any of them had thought to give the doctor a shot of the Ayahuasca he was studying. It might have made a difference. It had in his own case.

Aiden sat in his cage and watched, disgusted, as some of the female technicians walked by, still crying for the monster after three days. The man had killed dozens of men, heroes, but all he heard was how great of a man he had been, and oh, the loss...

Boo fucking hoo.

They needed to get the fuck out of there.

The best thing about Shu's death was that it proved a phenomenal distraction for their escape from the camp.

———

Late on the night of day four after Shu's death, Wulfe yelled at Aiden mentally.

American, Fontana says be ready. He heard one of the technicians talking and the Bitch in Blue arrives tomorrow to take over operations.

Aiden woke but didn't sit up in case someone was actually watching the security cameras. He wasn't surprised she was coming back, but he bet she was pissed. She'd made no secret of the fact that she hated the jungle. And if she was pissed off about returning it was hard to tell how their testing schedule would go.

It also made sense to leave now because they were the strongest they'd been in months. After a week without testing and the occasional double food ration from Smoke, they were as ready as they could be. They hadn't been out of their cages once in that time, and he was ready to move.

Excitement surged, and it was all he could do to roll over and pretend to sleep.

CHAPTER FOUR

Like a whisper, Fontana came for him two hours later, with Wulfe and TJ Rector by his side. *How the fuck did you get out of your cage?* Aiden demanded.

Fontana grinned and moved to the door. *Watch.*

Holding the iron lock in his hand, Fontana just looked at the thing for several seconds. Then, with a click, the lock fell open.

Aiden shook his head, amazed, and honestly a little fearful. Fontana was doing things he'd never even considered.

I managed to get the guards to fall asleep, Fontana told him. *We've got a little bit of time to get out of here. The cafeteria should be empty right now. I suggest we gather what food and water and supplies we can before we head out.*

Agreed.

We're not leaving.

Aiden's throat closed up as he stepped outside, unshackled and uncuffed for the first time in months. Yes, he was naked as a jaybird, but he was finally free. No one would be putting him back into handcuffs, he vowed. He would die first. Then what Wulfe said sank in, bringing him back to focus.

What are you thinking?

Wulfe looked at the medical building. *Our proof is there.*

The rest of them turned to look at the med center, knowing he was right. It housed all of the secrets. Shu had been meticulous about his notes, and they each had files several inches thick. The technicians had complained endlessly about the duplication. It could be a suicide mission going back in there, but they had no other option. Wulfe was right about that.

Rector and Fontana, go to the cafeteria and Shu's hut. See what you can find. We'll also probably need something to go through the fence, so look for some tools. Wulfe and I will see what we can find inside. Meet back here in thirty minutes.

The two men nodded and slipped away into the darkness. Aiden looked at Wulfe.

I really don't want to go in there, he admitted.

I don't also, but we must, American. This is the only time. She will get rid of everything. Every record, every note. And we will be liars.

Aiden knew he was right, but it didn't make it any easier to do. He scanned the area, checking for soldiers or guards, but the camp was deathly silent.

He looked at the squat cinder block building, fighting nausea. Deliberately, he slowed his breathing, but it was hard. His heart was trying to thud out of his chest and his body demanded oxygen. Aiden couldn't even remember how many dangerous missions he'd been on as a SEAL, but certainly into the triple digits. Too many to count. He'd been shot and stabbed, snake-bitten and had busted ankles and knees, and he'd take any one of those injuries again rather than voluntarily walk into that building.

Wulfe was thinking like a squad leader, though. They needed hard, physical proof of what had happened here. Otherwise everything they'd been through would be hearsay, unprovable.

Quietly, Aiden began gearing himself up, just like he did for hard assaults. Neither one of them was physically ready for hand to hand combat and they had no weapons other than their minds...but their fledgling abilities hadn't been tried in stressful situations. There was a very real chance that the first time he tried to *finesse* anyone they'd laugh in his face, then shoot him in the head. He was convinced that the sniper in the med center had been a fluke. The man had already wanted to kill— Aiden had just removed the tiniest restriction in his mind.

Wulfe slammed his doubled fists into Aiden's shoulders to psych him up and they turned toward the building.

They moved in the dark like wraiths, sliding from shadow to shadow. They would avoid all contact if possible and use all non-violent methods they could. If they alerted anyone, the gig would be up.

Pausing behind a clump of bushes about twenty-five feet away from the med center, Aiden looked at the soldiers guarding the door. He focused on the man on the right, pushing a feeling of tiredness. This was the farthest away he'd tried to do anything like this, so he didn't know how successful he'd be. The man was already leaning back against the wall, so it was easy enough to coax him to set his weapon aside and close his eyes. He murmured something to the second man, who nodded and watched as his partner squatted down and tipped his head back against the wall. Apparently, this was something they did regularly, swapping off to grab some sleep.

The first soldier closed his eyes and was asleep in seconds. The second soldier watched him for a long minute before a yawn split his own face. He widened his eyes and shifted his weapon in his arm, but Aiden could tell Wulfe was pushing power at him. Eventually, looking around at the dark, silent night, the second man sat on the ground and propped his elbow on his leg to support his head. The weapon went to the side to lean against the wall, just like the first soldier's.

The two of them gave the men ninety seconds to sleep before they started to creep forward.

The Silverstone Collaborative spent a lot of money on the camp, but even they couldn't control the lack of infrastructure this deep in the jungle. Power was hit and miss, so they'd installed a pretty significant generator system. They'd tried to secure the med center with keycard magnetic locks, but after overloading the system so many times they'd nixed the plan. Now it was an ordinary door, secured by Army soldiers.

Pausing at the entrance, they tried to feel if anyone was inside, but they couldn't feel anything. Everyone except Aiden's ragtag squad seemed to be sleeping exactly where they were supposed to be. Aiden twisted the lever handle and eased the door open, then waved Wulfe inside. Most of the overhead lights in the hallway were off, but there were small marker lights at the bottom edge of the hallways. It was just enough to illuminate their path. The knot in Aiden's stomach twisted tighter and tighter until he felt like he was about to throw up. Breathing through his nose he crouched low to move through the hallway. The muscles of his thighs were pumping with blood, and his body was pounding with health rather than sickness. If they'd been in any other situation he could have enjoyed the feeling. All of his old skills were coming back to him, but he knew his stamina was poor.

Aiden was sidetracked by a sign for the employee locker room. "Clothes," he hissed.

Wulfe nodded and they pushed into the room. There was

a bank of showers on one side of the room separated into male and female rooms, then two short walls of lockers. Aiden moved to these and started going through them, looking for anything they might be able to use in their escape. Within just a few minutes they had found more than enough of what they needed, plus several things he thought Fontana and Rector could use. They each found the white tech scrub pants to put on. Not the most tactical, of course, but anything was better than being naked with your dick swinging in the wind. Or being snake bait. Grabbing a duffel from the bottom of one of the lockers he threw in the clothes they'd gathered for Fontana and Rector. They also found a few pairs of white hospital shoes with Velcro. They must have belonged to the male orderlies. Aiden slipped a pair on, refusing to think about how ridiculous they would look tromping through the jungle. It would save their feet. Period.

Wulfe pulled him to a stop. "I'll go to the lab, and you go find Shu's office. Meet back here in a quarter hour."

Aiden gave him a mock salute and turned toward the only hallway he'd never been down. From what he'd seen, the med complex was built in a Y, with the research rooms on the right, and the offices on the left. As he maneuvered his way down the hallway, Aiden peered into the glass door of each office until he found one that had awards all over the wall. It had to be Shu's.

The door was locked. Fuck. He jiggled the handle and tried to feel with his mind how to work the tumblers of the lock. Fontana had opened the one on his cage earlier, and it seemed like it had been the thought of a moment. This one was just a door lock, nothing electronic, and as he felt out the pieces, he pushed on one that seemed to be in the way. Nothing happened. Turning, he stared at the piece of equipment blocking his way, focused, and imagined a finger *pushing* the tumbler back.

Something clicked inside the mechanism. Turning the handle, he pushed the door open. No fucking way... it had worked. There was no time to celebrate though. He had more to do.

There was a small lamp on a credenza to the left, but there were no exterior windows. Aiden flicked it on and looked around the room.

Dr. Edgar Shu had been a man of power. Over the years he'd accomplished many, many great things, and he'd gotten used to having money. It was obvious that the company had done everything it could to make his stay in this wild camp as comfortable as possible. It was bigger than any three of the other offices together he'd seen, and there was a comfortable looking couch along one wall, apparently for those nights that he didn't want to head back to his hut. The couch looked worn, like it had been slept on many times. The desk was a huge piece of mahogany, with two computer monitors. There were beautiful watercolors on the walls, the credenza that matched the desk, as well as a bank of several tall file cabinets.

Aiden scanned the room, wondering where he would even start.

Moving around behind the desk, he started going through drawers. He had no idea what exactly he was looking for, but surely there was something here.

In the right hand lower drawer of the cabinet, he found file folders on all of the current subjects. Flipping through them he found his own and started paging through the papers. Standard medical charts were on the top because they were the most recent. He flipped through the rest, finding a hand written 4x6 post-it-note in a scratchy hand.

Subject is a former Navy SEAL, hence incredibly resilient. Seems more resistant to injury than illness, exactly as a superlative soldier should be. Mentally, he's still fighting the restraints of captivity. I need to break him without killing him. Leverage brother?

Aiden's blood chilled in his veins. What did he mean, *leverage brother?* Aiden didn't have a brother, at least not that he knew of. Frustrated, he slapped the manila shut before he read further. He had no time.

Shaking his head, he set his folder, Wulfe's, Fontana's and Rector's on the desk, as well as several other names he remembered, then started searching again. In the center drawer was a set of keys, but they didn't appear to fit anything in the desk. He looked across at the file cabinets. Maybe those were locked. When he checked, the drawers slid open easily. Shu had apparently been a pretty trusting guy. No, that wasn't right. He wasn't here to lock everything up any more.

Before he delved into the file cabinets he wanted to look in the obvious places and see if there was a safe or something. Moving across the room he peered behind the watercolor of Chinese architecture. Nothing. Moving to the credenza he opened door and drawers, but again, nothing secure. He scanned the corners of the room, checked the tiles of the floor as well as the integrity of the walls, but there was no safe.

File cabinets, then.

There were three, so he started on the one on the right. Inside it was filled with folders. They were all neatly labelled with dates and the subject the experiment was taking place on. It looked like Shu had kept a file for every subject for every experiment. Damn, there were months of files in here. Leafing through, he looked for anything distinctive. There were a few red tabs. When he pulled those files, he realized that the experiment had resulted in death. Damn, there were so many red tabs.

Aiden continued to flip, looking for anything distinctive. He shuffled through the middle file cabinet, then moved to the one on the left. The top drawer was locked. Moving back to the center drawer of the desk he grabbed the keys in the tray. The lock on the drawer released as soon as he twisted the key. Inside, he found an expandable accordion file with the word Genesis across the front. Pulling it out Aiden released the elastic band from around the button.

Inside was a dark brown leather-bound journal. There was a rubber band looping around the cover and the pages within it. Aiden slipped off the band and started scanning the pages.

His gut bottomed out as he realized what he was looking at. This was the beginning. The genesis. On July 5th three years ago, Shu had written that an idea had come to him about a news article he'd read about the Amazonian jungle holy men and the plants they used. He wanted a retrieve a sample of the Ayahuasca root because he thought it might carry the same properties of another plant he was currently using in something called compound 6783. Aiden assumed that was one of his miracle drugs.

Paging through the book he stopped at an entry dated about thirteen months after the initial one. *Derivative is stronger than expected for primate subjects. 93% mortality rate after expanded mental growth. The Federal Drug Administration will not approve human testing.*

Aiden flipped through a few more pages. It was the entire history of Shu's program. Fuck, this was gold.

Aiden secured the band around the journal, then looked into the accordion file. A few loose-leaf pages of notes, a few Polaroid pictures, and at the very bottom, four black memory stick drives. They were only about two inches long and had the distinctive Silverstone Collaborative SC logo on one end. He prayed that they were as important as they appeared to be.

Shoving the file folders into the accordion file, he gathered it up into his arms. If they made it away, this would be the proof they needed to exonerate themselves for leaving if it came to that.

Aiden let himself out of the office and was about to return to Wulfe when he spied another door further down the hallway. Security. Curious, he headed that way. There could be weapons stashed here. When he very carefully tested the door knob, it turned easily. Cracking it, he listened, just to make sure there was no one there. Empty. He let himself into the office and looked around. There were banks and banks of monitors. All of the screens were split into nines, and as he looked, Aiden realized these were camera views of all of their cells, all of the research rooms, as well as every employee bungalow. Shu had apparently kept everyone under surveillance, not just the research subjects.

Looking around he realized that there was a bank of digital recorders behind him. Glancing at the monitors he looked a little more closely. Yep, there was the front entrance to the med center with the sleeping guards, and the Y of the hallway. If anyone rewound these recordings, they would see exactly who had escaped.

Wulfe, I need to destroy some equipment. I think they've been recording everything going on and it looks like it recorded us entering. I don't want any record of us being in this building tonight.

Agreed.

Any idea on how to do it without setting off alarms?

There was silence for a long moment. *No.*

Aiden tried to reach Fontana or Rector, but they were apparently too far away on the other side of the camp.

Wulfe, are you done?

Yes, American.

Head back to the meet up point. I'll give you ten minutes to find Fontana and Rector, then I'm torching this place. Anything less and it won't be enough to destroy all this.

Scheisse. We were supposed to sneak, American, not show them where we are.

If they see who broke in, they'll know exactly who to come after.

Aiden could almost hear him scowling on the other end of their connection. *Fine. Do it. Leaving now to find others.*

Then Aiden was alone in his mind.

CHAPTER FIVE

A iden tore the security room apart looking for anything usable for their escape. The security guards that worked inside the building carried small batons and cattle prods when they were moving the subjects between rooms or out to the Army men who escorted them to the cages. In a small room off the monitoring room, Aiden found a box of batons, as well as several charged cattle prods. The batons were okay, but they weren't ideal weapons. Neither were the cattle prods, but both might do in a pinch if they got into a scuffle.

There was a decent first aid kit, which he put onto his go pile, as well as a stack of black cargo pants with elastic waists. Stripping off the white scrubs he had on, he pulled on a pair of the cargos. Oh, fuck yeah. They felt like they were made for him. So much better than the scrubs they'd found. He went back into the room and found a stack of black t-shirts in plastic, as well. Ripping a couple out of the plastic, he pulled one on.

His normal size didn't fit. It kind of hung off the points of his shoulders. Shrugging, he tucked it into the waistband of the cargos and moved on. Then he looked at the plastic bags he'd ripped off. It would be smart to wrap everything they were taking in plastic. The Amazon basin was a rainforest and they received pelting downpours every day. It would suck to go to the trouble of stealing all this important stuff only to lose it because they hadn't taken care of it. Returning to the closet he looked for any other plastic, but the shirt wrappers seemed to be the only thing. He started ripping them open along the top seam and setting the t-shirts aside. Going to the duffel he'd found in the locker room, he removed all the white clothing, replacing it with black. Since there was still room in the duffel he rolled two white outfits together, then wrapped them in one of the plastic shirt wraps. That could be their backups.

Taking a moment, he also wrapped everything from the accordion file. The stick drives went into their own bag, and the journal went into its own bag, then the file folders. He twisted the tops into knots, hoping that it would be enough to keep them safe. And dry.

Time was slipping away. With a final mad scramble through the closet, he looked for anything they might possibly be able to use in the jungle. In one corner he found a white box full of six-inch twist flashlights. They weren't very big but in the depths of the jungle, any light would be welcome. He shoved a handful of them into the bag.

Nothing else caught his eye. Returning to the security room, he began tucking the white scrubs he wasn't taking between the equipment, then, using one of the cattle prods, he lit the fabric on fire. It almost seemed like there were too many electronics in here and nothing would burn, but it went up like a torch. Aiden watched for a long minute to make sure that it wasn't going to go out before he wrapped a wad of the burning fabric around the end of another prod and left the room, duffle over his shoulder. Jogging down the hallway he turned left at the Y and went to the locker room. There was a cart of laundry in one corner and he threw the burning cattle prod in there, then pushed the cart against several of the open lockers. It would burn.

Making sure the duffel was zipped, he put his arms through the handles and jogged back to the entrance to the med center. The door was propped open slightly with a piece of gravel. Thank you, Wulfe.

Aiden pulled the door open and slipped out. The two Brazilian Army soldiers still sat on the ground, sound asleep. One of the rifles was gone. Obviously Wulfe had taken it and left the other one for him. Aiden very carefully took the weapon up into his arms and headed back to the meet-up point.

Everyone was there waiting on him. Wulfe scraped mud onto the white fabric of the scrubs, but Aiden stopped him and shoved a bundle of clothes into his hands. *Cargos and a black t-shirt.* The other man began stripping immediately.

Fontana and Rector already had clothes on. They wore the rough linen clothing the locals preferred, as well as sandals. The shoes didn't quite fit Fontana's big feet, but they were close enough. Rector, on the other hand, had a more compact build and everything fit him perfectly. They were each carrying a large, bulging potato sack.

Aiden looked at Fontana but tried to include Rector. *The med center is about to go up. We need to get the fuck out of here.* He handed them each a cattle prod, a flashlight and a baton. There weren't enough guns to go around.

Both men took the weapons and Fontana took off into a jog. They all followed as quickly as they could in the dark. It was too soon to turn on the flash lights. *I cleared a path for us,* Fontana said, *and when they try to use their vehicles they may get a bit of a surprise.*

It felt good to stretch their legs in a run, but Aiden could immediately feel how out of shape he was. It had been almost a year since he'd been able to run this way. He wasn't the only one feeling the effects, though. They were all puffing by the time they reached the perimeter fence. If they faced any kind of serious pursuit, they would really have to work to get away. Plus, it was the middle of the night. There was no way they were going to cover as much ground as in the daytime.

As if in answer to his thoughts, the fire alarm went off in the camp. Aiden winced, wishing they'd had at least enough time to get through the fence.

Rector produced a pair of pliers and started cutting individual wires. It was slow and tedious work, but there was no way they could go over the fence. There were two curling ribbons of razor wire. If they'd been uniformed correctly they probably could have gone over it, but there was no way the cotton they wore would survive the razor blades, let alone their skin. And walking into the jungle with five hundred little cuts all over your body would be exceedingly dangerous.

Rector did a good job in cutting the corner, though. By the time they began to hear yelling voices, they were slipping through the gap in the fence. Once they were all through, Rector pulled the flap back down and secured it while Aiden covered him. Hopefully it would take the Army a while to find where they'd gone through.

Then they were trying to run through the jungle. Fontana had found some kind of long blade and he started hacking at the vegetation. Within just a few yards it was thick enough that they turned on the flashlights to see. Then, about a quarter mile from the fence, they found a faint game trail. Fontana ducked and started running, legs bent. He flashed hand signals when he thought they needed to see something. Occasionally it opened up and they could stand vertically. Other times they had to slow to a crawl because they couldn't find a way through the wall of green.

Rector lagged behind and Aiden paused. "Are you okay?" he hissed.

"Yeah, just so damn out of shape."

Nodding, Aiden waved him ahead. He would bring up the rear for a while.

The flashlights were enough to illuminate what was exactly in front of you, but no more than that. They listened for the sound of pursuit, but it never came. They had debated following the road out of the camp but decided against it. If anyone saw them and were beholden to the camp for anything, there was a chance they would be reported. So, following a game trail, they wound away from the camp. After about an hour Fontana called a halt.

They were all out of breath. Aiden leaned against a tree with no thorns and braced his hands on his knees. His heart was going to thud right out of his chest. As he looked at the lush landscape around him, though, he decided if he had to die it could be in a place like this. At least it wouldn't be in a cell, or on a damn stainless steel medical table they could just wash the blood off of when they were done.

Fontana produced a blue, multi-folded, laminated map and spread it open across the ground. "I don't know exactly where we are, but I think we're somewhere in this area. The tech I asked had no real idea." He pointed to a broad expanse of green with very few dividing lines or identifiable roads. "It looks like the shortest possible distance to the coast, where we'll be able to arrange pickup, hopefully, is to head northeast."

His finger followed a line to the coast, and Aiden's heart sank. He had hoped that they would be at least near some city, but it didn't appear that they were. It would take weeks to reach the coast, especially if they had to navigate thick vegetation. If by chance they found a village they might be able to focus in on where they were, and maybe find transportation. If they had to hike that entire way, though, it would take them weeks to get anywhere.

He had thought that getting away from the camp might be the hardest part, but now he wasn't so sure.

———

They agreed to head northeast, then they started going through their bags and cataloging everything they had. Fontana had broken into one of the American tech's rooms who had been known for being an outdoorsman and had a treasure trove of equipment.

"The guy started to wake up and I told him to go back to sleep and dream about women with big tits. He smiled as he drifted off."

They all laughed because they all wished they could do that, and it was the perfect way to break the ice after their escape.

Fontana had hit the jackpot though. In an excess of preparedness, the tech had brought along a bunch of camping supplies. Not especially useful in the Amazon jungle, but maybe it could be. There was a backpack with a mosquito net, a machete, a firestarter, and a weird straw thing that you could apparently drink through that would filter the water before it made it to your mouth. There was a length of fishing line with a small hook, possibly usable if they hit one of the Amazon's many tributaries. Rope.

"How did you know he had this stuff?" Aiden asked.

"During one of the tests he was bitching at himself at how much money he'd spent on all the camping gear when he hadn't used any of it. Apparently, the camp was enough for him and he had no desire to go beyond the perimeter fence. I think he was scared shitless when he got a look at the jungle."

Aiden shook his head as he played his flashlight over all

the gear. That was probably right. This was an urban outfitter's overpriced gear pack, but it was better than nothing.

TJ Rector displayed the food he'd managed to gather. There were a few cans of smoked meat, vegetables and fruit, as well as several packets of freeze dried vegetables. A bag of sugar packets as well as a bag of salt packets. That was good because they would need the salt with the way they were sweating. There was a box of crackers as well as what appeared to be a cheesecloth wrapped package of meat. Hm. That might be kind of iffy unless they ate it soon. He'd also gathered several plastic wrapped packages of the oat cakes they all knew and loved.

Aiden winced but he knew they would need the calories to get through the jungle.

Wulfe brought out his haul next. He'd been carrying a black box and when he opened it, Aiden recognized the bottles of Ayahuasca serum that the doctor had produced. Two of the bottles were partially drained, but a third was completely full. He stared at the drug for a long time, not sure exactly how he felt about it.

"Seemed foolish to leave it," Wulfe said simply, and they all nodded.

Once they'd catalogued everything they had they shared part of a liter bottle of water, then took off again. The going was slow. And dangerous. Aiden brought up the rear and his flashlight beam caught several dangerous critters moving across their path. He paused once to look at the paw prints of some type of cat, probably a jaguar. When he spread his fingers over the impression, they barely reached the edges.

"Maybe we're too scrawny to appeal to him," TJ murmured, catching sight of the tracks. Aiden snorted, but he wasn't so sure.

In spite of their tiredness they managed to travel for several hours. Fontana, the most knowledgeable about jungle terrains, called a halt in a small clearing. "I think we should take a break, rehydrate and catch some sleep. As soon as the Bitch in Blue gets to the camp she's going to be after us. I'll take first watch."

Aiden thought that was a brilliant plan. Moving to some kind of little palm tree, he broke off a couple of long fronds and laid them on the ground. Sitting on the fronds he pulled off the once white nurse shoes to let them dry. Then, curling up with his head on his elbow, he drifted off to sleep. It was the best mattress he'd had in months and he slept like the dead.

———

They each grabbed three hours of sleep, then they split a bottle of water and each ate one of the calorie dense oatcakes.

Just after dawn they heard the sound of a helicopter heading for the camp. It wasn't directly overhead but definitely close enough that they gave in to the urge to take cover. "Heads are going to be blown off," Wulfe murmured.

Yes, that tended to be how Bitch in Blue handled so many issues. Or with that handy stiletto of hers through the brain, à la Captain Aguirre.

Aiden didn't feel bad for any of the people in that camp though. Everyone had seen the men in the cages and done nothing about it. They'd never reported anything and no one had ever come to check on the men being housed so cruelly. Fuck them all.

"Fuck 'em all," Fontana snapped, echoing Aiden's thoughts. "They deserve everything coming to them."

Wulfe looked back toward the direction of the camp, but there was no way he could see anything now. They were at least several miles away.

"We need to go," Rector said, his voice quavering just the tiniest bit. "That woman is not getting her hands on me again."

They packed up their few belongings and headed out, following a machete-swinging Fontana. The straps of the bag had left abrasions on his shoulders, but he wasn't complaining. He was too happy to be gone.

———

They came across their first village three days later. They scoped it out for two hours before deciding that things seemed to be fairly quiet. The villagers appeared to be poor farmers, making do with what they could cultivate from the land. Brown-skinned, dark-haired children ran around playing, with the elderly adults looking on from the shade of a hut. It was midday and the heat had become sweltering. Younger men and women were in the fields the team could see cleared on the other side of the village. There was a slight track to the village, but no vehicles.

"Is it even worth stopping?" Fontana growled. "It's too small to be on the map and people like this would love to sell the Collaborative information about us. Hell, if the army comes they won't even bargain, they'll just tell them."

He was probably right, but Aiden needed to know that they were heading in the right direction.

"They might be able to tell us how to get to one of the villages actually on the map," TJ suggested.

Wulfe, a frown darkening his beard-grizzled face, nodded once. "I think, even with danger, we should get idea of location."

So, over Fontana's scowling objections, they decided to go forward and see if they could discover their location. Rector was voted the ambassador, because he supposedly spoke fluent Portuguese. Aiden would believe that when he saw it.

"Give me that lame ass camping bag," he told them. Fontana handed it over.

The kid seemed dismayed that he'd volunteered the information but, firming his shoulders, he headed down the slight incline and into the village. Aiden didn't think they had a choice. They had to know where they were.

As soon as he entered the clearing tension ran through the people of the village. An older woman stood up and called the children in, obviously telling them to hurry because they ran like their hair was on fire. TJ tried to look harmless, but he was too obviously military in bearing to do that. He was also obviously white, so the people were leery. He spoke several words in Portuguese and one woman gave him a terse answer. He asked another question and she murmured to the older man beside her, then she shouted out the answer. TJ repeated it incredulously, and the woman nodded firmly.

Reaching into the bag carefully, one hand up in a calming gesture, he lifted out two of the flashlights and flicked them on to show that they were still usable. He called out a few words, but the woman shook her head vehemently, crossing her arms over her chest. He was trying to barter for food, but the woman was not willing to budge. She spewed something at him, and TJ bowed his head to her, then turned to leave.

One of the more daring children had crept to the closest corner of a building to TJ, where the woman couldn't see. The boy seemed fascinated as he looked TJ up and down, then looked at the flashlight in his hand. The sun had risen, but it was still possible to see the light when he turned it on and shone it at the boy. The child, who couldn't have been more than ten, gasped. It was apparent he wanted to come near but it was equally apparent that he was scared spitless of the domineering old woman.

TJ turned off the light and tossed it to the boy, who caught it in his hands. Then he found the button and turned the light on, racing back to his friends to show them the prize for being daring.

Aiden wanted to laugh at the boy's antics. The batteries in that thing would be dead in no time if he kept it on all day. But that light may have saved their lives at some point. Yes, they had several, but it was hard to know what they faced ahead.

With a final wave at the people, TJ turned to head back into the jungle. He was almost at the forest line when the woman called out a word, stopping him in his tracks. She strode out to him, proud in her threadbare t-shirt and colorful skirt, and handed him a small, rag-wrapped bundle. Then she murmured a few quiet words to him before turning and heading back to her people.

TJ bowed to her in thanks, then turned and headed into the bush. They didn't talk as they met up, just headed through the jungle for a while. Once Fontana thought they were far enough away, they crouched down together.

"What did she tell you?" Aiden asked.

"We're in a reserve on the southern side of the Amazon River. And we're about three hundred miles from the closest decent sized port where we can find a phone or an airport or anything. She says there's another small village along a road if we head directly east, and sometimes there's a truck there, but it's no guarantee." He looked down at the package in his hands and unwrapped the fabric. Inside were several pieces of cooked meat. Aiden hoped it was chicken. TJ split the meat between them all, then broke off pieces of the banana the woman had wrapped as well. It was a filling meal, and surprisingly good.

"I could feel how leery she was of me, even fearful. It took a lot of courage for her to approach me, and the closer she got the more scared she became. But she managed it."

"We might encounter a lot of that on our way out of here," Fontana said thoughtfully. "We look military and I doubt they have reason to trust anyone in the military, *any* military."

The others nodded. It would probably be smart to work on walling themselves off from that kind of emotion. They couldn't afford to be overwhelmed by other people's joys or fears. In this part of the world, Aiden was sure there was more worry and fear and desperation than joy.

As soon as they'd started making contact with each other in the camp, Aiden noticed that they were picking up a kind of static from other people as well, and he received general mood impressions. It was distracting to say the least. A couple of times Aiden had picked up impressions strong enough to almost respond to the person actually having the feelings. When he'd asked Wulfe about it, he'd admitted that he'd been having the same issues. Apparently, in addition to the Ayahuasca strengthening their bodies, it seemed to be opening multiple pathways in their minds as well.

After their meal they hunkered down against trees and took a sweaty nap, waving tenacious bugs away. Aiden was covered in welts from insect bites, but there wasn't much he could do about it other than wave them away and be eaten.

They were startled awake by gunfire. Aiden scrambled to his feet immediately, weapon held at the ready. The gunfire, though faint, was probably more than two miles away, back in the direction of the village they'd just left. They looked at each other in grim knowledge.

"We have to go back," TJ said, fists clenching and unclenching.

"If we go back, we get shot as well. We move out," Fontana said firmly. He turned for the forest and started hacking his way through the vegetation. "They're going to be on our tails if we don't move our asses right now."

Unfortunately, TJ was overruled and they headed out, following Fontana. Aiden's chest ached at the thought of the Brazilian Army moving in on the poor village. There had been too many shots for it to be random firing. The Army had a hint of their whereabouts now, and they would capitalize on that.

But *how* had they gotten their whereabouts? Finding one small random village in the Amazon basin was ridiculously precise. They had to have been tracking them.

"Wait guys. Hold up."

"We don't have time, Will," Fontana snapped, using the shortened version of Willingham. All of the guys had begun using the shortened version.

"We have to," he said firmly. "How did they know we were in the village?"

The three men looked at each other for a long second, then back to Aiden. "Tracker," Wulfe said with a snarl.

"I don't think it's anything we grabbed, though."

They blinked at each other again. "American, you think inside us?"

He nodded at Wulfe. "As much as we've been poked and prodded, you know they could have slipped a tracker in us easily."

Fontana looked down at himself grimly. "I can't even tell you how many cuts and gouges I've had in the past year."

Aiden couldn't either. "They would want it on the same place on every person. Look for scars in the same place."

TJ found it a few minutes later. There was a scar just under his clavicle, as well as on all three other men. When they palpated the site, they could feel something rolling beneath the skin.

"That has to be it," Aiden told them. Scrambling for the first aid kit, he dug through the contents. He found the scalpel blade first, then the handle, and snapped them together. Then, using an antibacterial wipe, he started scrubbing a clean spot onto TJ's skin. "You better sit down, buddy."

TJ gritted his teeth and sank down onto a fallen log. As he laid back on the thing, Aiden could see how white the younger soldier had turned. "I'll be as quick as possible," he promised.

He had to be, because he was fairly certain he could hear yelling coming toward them.

Using a finger, he palpated the area again, then pulled the scalpel from the plastic sleeve. With a decisive cut, he split TJ's skin just beneath his clavicle. Dragging air through his clenched teeth, the Ranger didn't say a word, though Aiden knew it had to hurt like a bitch. After making a half inch incision, he worked the blade down inside, feeling something hard at the tip. Digging a little, he forced up a small, white plastic tube, about the size of a large piece of rice. Was that seriously it?

Aiden set the tracker onto a piece of plastic, then put a wad of gauze over TJ's cut. "Sit there a minute and I'll bandage it."

Fontana was next, gritting his teeth as Aiden made a similar cut almost directly over the old scar. His tracker almost popped out, no digging required. He made Fontana hold a gauze piece over his wound.

Wulfe was waiting on Fontana's other side. Aiden made the cut and squeezed, and the small tracker popped right out. He put it on the piece of plastic beside the others and made Wulfe hold gauze to the incision. Then, going back to TJ, he positioned a butterfly bandage over the cut, then a waterproof Band-Aid over the whole thing. Then he did the same to the other two men. Then, handing the scalpel to Wulfe handle first, he took their place on the log.

Wulfe gave him a dangerous grin as he leaned over him, his vibrant blue eyes flashing, but he did the job as quickly as Aiden had. Then he applied the same care. They were done within about five minutes. Aiden looked down at the four little white cylinders. "That's what they were following."

"Bastards," Fontana growled. "Throw them under the log and let's get the fuck out of here. They're getting closer. I have *never* wanted a block of C4 as bad as I do right this minute. I would booby-trap that shit in a nanosecond."

Aiden threw the locators under the log and they took off again. Even knowing they were being chased, it was still slow going. Every step they made had to be fought for; the Amazon jungle didn't just let you walk through her depths.

Fontana found another game trail and was able to stop using the machete. In a crouching run they made better time, until they hit a tributary. Veering north, he followed the heavy stream until it disappeared into the earth. They'd come across several springs like this, pushing out enough water to drown a man, then disappearing into the forest floor. They circled the spring and kept going.

They slogged for a solid three miles before Wulfe pulled them to a stop. The sun had faded below the canopy and night was beginning to fall. "I think they pull back now."

As soon as they stopped, TJ sank to the ground and pulled out the rag the woman had given them.

"You can't feel bad about that, TJ," Aiden told him. "We had no idea they would track us there."

TJ shook his head. "I know, Will," he admitted. "I'm just tired of all the killing. I got into the Rangers to help people, you know?"

"We all did, American," Wulfe told him quietly.

"It's that Bitch in Blue," Fontana said. "She's not going to let up until she finds us. And if she figures out we stole information about the Spartan Project before you torched the place, we're going to be in even more shit. She's smart enough that she's going to assume worst case scenario, just like we would."

"We're like dogs to her," TJ said softly, his dark eyes full of bitterness. "They had us chained up and now they're looking to recover us, their property. She even put a damn locator on us. But now that we've bitten her she'll probably try to put us down."

Aiden nodded. "She'll definitely try."

The four of them looked at each other and nodded once.

"Do we have specifics on the program?"

Aiden nodded. "From the beginning. Personal, hand-written notes. And files on the subjects."

"Did you grab those?"

Aiden nodded again and swung the pack around. The plastic wrapped accordion file was on the bottom of the bag and it had stayed dry so far. Unwrapping the plastic as carefully as he could so that he could use it again, he opened the flap and pulled out the manila personnel folders. Each man got their own folder and Aiden had to admit he was damn curious about the info in his. He started flipping through pages.

"They told my mother I was dead," TJ told them, his voice numb.

They all had a notation like that. *Family notified killed in Training accident*. What bastards.

Whoever had investigated them had done a very good job. Aiden read his own bio dispassionately. The only thing that shocked him was seeing his old name.

James David Rogers, born to single mother. Father unknown. One sibling, male. Mother surrendered parental rights of sibling at age 5.

Surrendered parental rights of James at age 4. No known familial
contact. Mother deceased three years later, drug overdose.

Ward of the State of Maryland for thirteen years. Occasional
shifts to foster care, but no lasting placements. Graduated Garfield
High School at seventeen. Officially changed name to Aiden David
Willingham on 18th birthday. Joined US Navy two weeks later.

He skimmed the rest, not seeing any other pertinent info.

"This is so messed up," Fontana groused, paging through
his file.

Aiden handed him the leather journal. "No, this is
messed up."

Every half-baked experiment Shu's brain had cooked up
was here. The flavor of the words conveyed that he was
excited to be working on human subjects. This was his
personal view on everything. There were doodles and
scratches, plans for equipment he needed to build.

Aiden looked at the men grouped around him. When
they'd had their initial meeting in Washington, he'd seen
Fontana but he hadn't had a chance to introduce himself. The
other SEAL had been big and broad, with wildly curling dark
blond hair and a darker beard. He'd also been one of the most
brash and charismatic in the group, telling raunchy jokes and
drawing men to him.

The first time Aiden had seen Rector he'd been being
dragged toward the med center, one of the guards using the
cattle prod on him when he wouldn't move. Stocky and well-
built with dark eyes, he'd seemed young and fiery. Aiden
assumed his hair was normally dark, because he'd had dark
chest and pubic hair, but the man's head had been freshly
shaven.

They'd all been shaved when they'd first arrived, and
stripped. It had been the first of many humiliations.

Wulfe was another he hadn't seen until they'd been at the
camp for a couple months. Another subject had been in that

cage, but he'd died. Then Wulfe had been moved in, a strapping German spewing creative epithets. The hired muscle hadn't known what he'd been saying, but Aiden knew enough slang to get by, and it made him laugh.

As he looked at the men now, he realized how much the camp had taken out of them. They'd all lost weight, yes, but it was more than that. The dogged humor had left Wulfe's pale eyes, and Fontana didn't have the same confidence he once did. Neither did TJ, for that matter.

But today there was gritty determination in all of their expressions, and it made him proud to be with them. Even if they got caught tomorrow, he was glad he'd been part of this group.

Fontana shook his head as he flipped through the pages. In disgust he tossed the book to Wulfe to look through. The older man's mouth tightened but he went through every page, scanning carefully, then passed the book on.

"I found his phone," Fontana told them, pulling it from his pocket, "but there's no service out here of course."

"We should wrap that in plastic, American. Take the battery out of it so they can't locate it."

Fontana handed it to Aiden who took the pieces apart, buried it into the dry clothes roll, then sealed it up again. So far everything was staying dry, even though they'd had rain every day. When the storm clouds moved in they could find cover beneath some of the flora, the leaves as long and broad as a person. If they had to go through one of the rivers, they might be fucked.

They slogged through the jungle for days without seeing even a hint of another person or any hint of civilization. The Amazon rainforest was so dense, so remote, they felt almost as isolated from the rest of the world as they'd been in the cages. They bedded down at night and tried to recover the health they'd lost. Food was becoming an issue, though. They were used to going without, so it wasn't like they were eating a lot, but four mouths consumed a fair amount of food quickly, even when they were trying to be frugal. Water wasn't as much of an issue. They'd managed to catch a few rainfalls to replenish the water bottles but the forest made them work for everything else.

Aiden was desperately hungry. They were burning more calories than they were taking in, so they were always at a deficit and didn't have any reserves to count on.

When Aiden had gone through training, he'd been shown what critters were edible and which would make you sicker than a dog or kill you, but that had been several years ago. They still had the guns but shooting at a wild pig or monkey might alert the wrong people to their location. They would only do that if their situation turned dire. For now, they would ration the food and water.

Three days later their situation turned dire.

CHAPTER SIX

They were plowing through the jungle like they had been when they began to climb a fairly steep slope. It had been raining on them all day, a constant downpour. Some of the drops hitting Aiden's head felt like ping pong balls. He glanced around, something bothering him.

Hey, guys, hold up.

They all stopped and stood in the downpour, looking at Aiden.

What is it?

I'm not sure. Something just doesn't feel right.

They waited for several long moments, brushing water from their faces as they peered into the murk. He felt ridiculous when nothing presented.

Let's go, Wulfe murmured.

Fontana checked his direction, then continued chopping at the dense vegetation. He suddenly paused and turned to them. "Hey, I think I hear..."

Then he was gone, the ground giving way beneath him.

"Fontana!"

Aiden stopped several feet from where his fellow SEAL had disappeared.

Fontana! Wulfe called.

They all waited to hear the response, but nothing came. Aiden crept up the path Fontana had cleared and immediately saw where the ground had softened from the rain and given way beneath him in a giant mudslide. Aiden backed up, not wanting to be the next to go over. "Do we have a rope in that pack?"

TJ pulled the pack from his shoulders and pulled the red nylon rope out, tossing it to Aiden.

"I'll go over and try to find him. I can't see through the vegetation where he went. If you guys want to head down and around, maybe find an easier path."

The men nodded.

Aiden tied the rope off to a tree, then fashioned a rope harness to go around his lower body. If he did this right he could control the slack as he went down and the others could retrieve the rope when he hit bottom.

TJ and Wulfe made sure he was as secure as possible before they took off downhill.

It had been a while since Aiden had done rope work, but when your ass was on the line things usually came back to you pretty easily. He rappelled down the steep hill, going as fast as he dared. It was worrying that there had been no response from Fontana. Either he was too far away or he was unconscious.

In some sections he had decent footing, but there were steep areas where he was literally hanging only by the rope itself. There were divots in the mud where it looked like Fontana had hit, then kept sliding. After rappelling almost a hundred and fifty feet, the ground began to even out. A fast-moving stream tumbled over rocks just a few yards away. Then he found Fontana.

There was blood and mud all over him and most obvious a horrendously broken right leg. It was laying twisted beneath him, with an open compound fracture of the lower leg. Aiden went to his knees in the dirt, feeling for a pulse. It was there, but when he peeled back Fontana's eyelids, his pupils responded unevenly. That was not a good sign.

"Hey, buddy. I know you're hardheaded enough to survive this, but why don't you open your eyes and show me you're still here."

No response.

Wulfe and TJ arrived just a few minutes later. TJ looked at the open fracture and had to turn away. Aiden didn't have the option.

"We have to get this wound clean," he told Wulfe. "And try to get the leg set before he comes around."

With a grim nod, Wulfe looked around the scene. "We have some bottle water, but not enough."

Aiden sat back on his heels. "Stream water?"

Wulfe shrugged. "Infection will set in no matter what we do."

Yes, that was very true. Aided had gotten a small cut on his hand going through the fence that had become infected almost immediately. It had taken a day to seal up properly.

"TJ, start making camp and if you can manage it, start a fire. We're going to be here a while."

TJ winced, obviously aware of how difficult it was to start a fire with damp material all around them. They were deep inside a rainforest, so they hadn't had a fire since they'd left the camp. If they were here for any length of time, though, they would need to start boiling water.

Aiden noticed spreading blood beneath Fontana's hip. "Wulfe, we need to get him straight and I need to see where that blood is coming from."

Immediately, Wulfe moved down Fontana. Very carefully,

Aiden rocked Fontana's body toward him, allowing Wulfe to pull the leg straight. Nausea churning his stomach as he heard the bones grind together, Aiden forced himself to look beneath Fontana. The machete was buried in his ass cheek.

"Are you fucking kidding me?"

He looked at it for a long minute.

"What do you think?"

Pull it out, Wulfe told him bracingly. *Sooner it's out the sooner it can heal.*

Without hesitation Aiden pulled the twelve-inch knife from Fontana's ass. It had cut into the flesh lengthwise in about an eight-inch gash and bled heavily when he first removed it.

We need to get him into the water and get everything flushed.

Nodding, Aiden moved to remove the clothes from his friend's lower half. He had to cut the pants off. Then, wedging his arms beneath Fontana's armpits from behind, Wulfe moved to his hips.

One, two, three...

Damn, he's heavier than he looks.

Moving in tandem, he and Wulfe carried Fontana down the bank to the flowing water, the broken leg swinging nauseatingly. The stream was only about ten feet across, but it seemed to be moving pretty fast. The stiff current pulled on his legs.

"Any chance we're going to call piranha to us?"

He'd been joking but Wulfe peered into the dark water. "I don't think so. It's not a big enough tributary to support them."

They waded into the water till they were waist deep and slowly let Fontana drift with the current. He gasped at one point but didn't regain consciousness. Aiden kept talking to him mentally anyway, letting him know that they were taking care of him. They let him float for a half-hour to let the water rinse away the dirt that had been on the ends of the protruding bone. When they carried him up the bank and back to the campsite, they found TJ had spread a Mylar emergency blanket along the ground. That was smart thinking. At least now they wouldn't re-contaminate the wounds.

Some of the skin around the right lower leg break had already started to repair itself. "I think we need to set his leg first. It's going to be a bitch."

Wulfe nodded and moved to Fontana's feet.

"TJ, we're going to need your help."

TJ came over but refused to look at the damaged area. "What do you need?"

"If you can pull on his shoulders, Wulfe will pull on the broken leg and we'll try to get the two pieces to fit together."

The younger man cringed but gritted his teeth and moved to Fontana's head. "I'll do it."

Aiden dug through the first aid kit in his duffle but there was nothing big enough to splint a lower leg. He looked around, debating what he could use. There was wood everywhere. He might just have to chop off a couple of small branches with the machete. He picked up the blood-soaked blade and moved to a tree, selecting a limb to hack down. He could split this one into two pieces. Once he was ready he moved back to the blanket and their wounded man.

Fontana looked pale in the dimness of the forest. The rain had finally begun to let up, giving them some relief. Aiden drew out several heavy-duty gauze pads, as well as a roll of fabric tape. If they could get this sealed, hopefully his Ayahuasca enhanced body would take over the rest. "Okay, on my mark you guys need to pull with everything you have."

He sat on his knees and drew in a deep breath. This was not going to be easy.

Pull, he told the men.

Fontana cried out in pain, but Aiden didn't stop. When

the pulling wasn't enough to get the bones ends together, he reached in with his hands to line them up. Throughout all his years, he'd never done anything as difficult as match up the two ends of bone. He gagged a couple of times but refused to let himself puke. Finally, they snapped together like two pieces of a puzzle. Aiden drew his hands back slowly, making sure they were going to stay together. They did. Moving as quickly as he dared, he disinfected the open wound then bandaged it. Then, while the men kept tension on the leg, he splinted it.

It was a nasty piece of work when they were done, but it seemed like it was going to hold.

"Roll him over. Let's get it all done."

The wound from the machete was trying to seal itself, but it was so long that Aiden was worried that it would take too long and infection would set in. Flushing the gash with disinfectant, he started pulling the sides together and using tape to secure them.

"Buddy, you are so going to owe me," Aiden growled.

When he was done, the wound had stopped bleeding and the sides were as aligned as possible.

"I think we should give him a dose of the serum. It might be enough to boost him."

Wulfe nodded and moved to the stream to wash his hands. They all did, then they returned to what would be their camp for a few days.

The serum boost seemed to help, but Fontana still developed a fever. Aiden had expected that. He'd had dirt in the open break and they'd rinsed it with murky river water. And it was hard to tell what might have been on the machete blade when it sank into his ass.

Wulfe managed to get a fire going with deadwood he'd

found near the stream and they'd finally been able to boil water. As Fontana had shuddered with cold, they'd managed to get some warm water down him. Then the delusions had started. He'd never roused to complete consciousness, but he'd come to enough to know there were shapes moving around him that he couldn't identify. All three of them had talked to him both mentally and verbally, but it hadn't helped. He kicked his legs out and Aiden feared he would hear the bone in Fontana's leg snap apart, but it never did.

Eventually they were all on the ground with him, keeping hands on him and talking to him to keep him calm. Aiden understood his fear. More than once the orderlies had held him down and forced things on him that he wasn't able to fight. For a man who had been trained to be indestructible, it was a deafening blow to the ego.

After a few hours Fontana roused a little. "What the fuck did you people do to me?"

Aiden leaned over him so that he could see his eyes. "You did it to yourself, buddy. Tried a mudslide with no seatbelt."

"Huh," he murmured, drifting back to sleep.

On the second day they heard a helicopter approaching.

"Put the fire out!" Wulfe hissed.

They scrambled to smother the fire with big armfuls of dirt. It sat smoldering for a few minutes, just long enough for the helicopter to fly over top of them. Once it was gone, none of them moved to light the fire again until Fontana began to shiver.

"Think it was the Bitch?" TJ asked.

Aiden nodded. "Definitely."

They kept watch over Fontana for three days before he managed to sit up and talk to them. The leg seemed to be healing, though it was an angry red all around the break. His ass, on the other hand, had healed perfectly, though there was a bit of a pinch of skin on one end where Aiden hadn't gotten the sides perfectly aligned. He would have a scar, but it didn't seem to hurt him when he sat up.

Fontana drank more water and ate some food, then went back to sleep.

"When do you think he'll be able to travel," Wulfe murmured.

Aiden shrugged. "A couple days probably, and then only part of the day, I would think. That was a devastating injury. It's not healing great."

Wulfe nodded, whittling a piece of wood with the long knife. They had settled into a routine in the camp. TJ maintained the fire while Aiden and Wulfe gathered the wood, and whatever protein they managed to find. The stream had proven to be full of small fish, just the right size to skewer and roast over the fire. Aiden was glad to have real cooked food, even if it was a little bland.

They took shifts to guard at night, but they hadn't seen any kind of habitation or even human movement at all. TJ had climbed to the top of the incline to reconnoiter, but there was nothing other than jungle canopy. No smoke, no breaks in the tree lines where roads might be, nothing. When he'd returned he'd seemed a little pissed off. Aiden could feel the desperation and frustration rolling off of him.

"We'll make it out of here, TJ."

The other man had shaken his head and slicked back his short dark hair. "It doesn't seem like there's any end to it. How do we know we're even heading in the right direction?"

Aiden motioned to the sky. "We know where the sun rises every morning. That tells us which direction we're heading."

As an Army Ranger, TJ actually had more frontiering training than Aiden did, but he didn't have the confidence most Rangers had. Aiden tried to reinforce him, but a lot of that would have to come with age, and accomplishments. Or maybe he'd had it but Shu had taken it from him. TJ had only been in the Rangers about five years before he signed up for the Spartan Project.

On the fourth day after Fontana's injury, he got up and walked. There was a significant limp, but it held him long enough to get him to the stream to wash off four days of body muck. Wulfe waded in with him just to be sure he didn't drift away, but Fontana waved him off. "I'm good. Yes, it's achy, but it definitely doesn't feel like it was broken. More like a heavy bone bruise from a car crash or something."

That was amazing. The break had been the worst injury TJ, Aiden and Wulfe had ever seen, and Fontana didn't even remember it.

"Do you remember me digging the machete out of your ass?" Aiden joked.

Fontana looked at him for a long moment before shaking his head. "No. And I don't want to."

They feasted on the little silver *aracu* bait fish that night, then woke the next day and broke camp. They had debated staying one more night, but Wulfe and Aiden both felt something oppressive coming from the west. They weren't sure what, but it was motivating them to move.

TJ had found a spot where the stream narrowed and they crossed. Aiden took the lead, swinging the machete from side to side. It was hard going because of the vegetation and his inexperience in hacking at it, but after a while he learned how to maximize the damage his swings did. He wasn't as good as Fontana by any means, but the other man seemed content to follow, his limp growing more pronounced as the day wore on.

When the sky opened up on them about midday, they decided to take a break. They could barely see each other ten feet away through the downpour. Finding a broad-leafed plant, Aiden dropped down to the ground beneath it.

The rain combined with the humidity made everything

miserable. More often than not they slogged with damp clothes binding in the cracks and bends of their bodies. They'd made sure to keep all of the paper items they'd stolen from the camp sealed into the plastic bags for security reasons, and so far everything seemed to be holding.

They'd only traveled a few miles before they had to call a halt. Fontana tried to protest but Aiden could see the pain in his face. "We'll make it up another day," he told the man.

That night they each had an oat cake. After a week of being on the run, about half of their food was gone. They'd rationed as much as they could and supplemented with the fish, but they were still putting out far more calories than they were taking in. They needed a large source of protein. With that thought in mind, after they'd made camp, Aiden set out to hunt.

If you fire that weapon, Wulfe warned, *they will find us.*

I don't think so.

But he took the machete with him just in case he found something else.

Aiden walked for miles, it seemed like, the clothing dragging on his body as it showered, then cleared. He dodged a huge spider web and saw the tail end of a coral snake disappear into the brush. He debated snatching for it because it would be a good source of protein, but he'd tangled with venom before and he had no desire for a rematch.

They weren't staying long enough for him to set a trap, but maybe if he could set a snare they could check it in the morning on the way out. This was to the east of camp and they would be headed in this general direction tomorrow. Besides, he'd already reconned the path.

Using a short length of the nylon rope he'd cut off, he found a decent game trail. A sapling just to the left of the trail would serve as his spring. Finding a couple of sturdy little branches, he worked them down with the machete into the configuration needed to set the snare. He didn't have any bait, so he would have to rely on the snare itself to set off the spring.

Pretty iffy odds hoping a critter would stick his head through this little tiny loop of line.

It was what he would hope for though.

There was nothing in the snare the next day. Fontana managed to walk a little further, but still needed to pull up early. Aiden went out with his snare pieces and set up another trap.

When they passed by it the next morning, it wasn't tripped either. So, he dismantled the pieces and packed them in his bag.

Their food was running dangerously low. They were down to half a dozen oat cakes. Even if they only ate half of the oatcake per person, that would only feed them for three days.

They needed actual food.

Wulfe had tried some of the plants to see if they were edible, but they had left him doubled over in pain in the bush. They couldn't afford to be too picky, but if it was going to set them back from where they were, it wasn't worth the risk.

It was TJ that got them food the next night. They'd stopped to bed down for the night and he'd gone off to piss. He didn't realize he'd parked himself over top of a boa constrictor hidden in the knee of a tree until the animal moved.

When he walked back into the camp with the six-foot animal hanging limp from his hand they all cheered. Aiden immediately started gathering fire material. Wulfe cleared out an area for the camp. They would be staying for a while now, and Fontana guided TJ in how to skin and dress the reptile.

The fire was a bitch to start. They finally resorted to using one of the manila folders, stuffing the papers into another folder. The meat was only good for so long, and it was a huge source of protein for them. Finding material to feed the fire was difficult, but they persevered, drying wood by the fire to be burned later. Finally, they wrapped the clean stretch of meat around a tree branch and began to roast it.

It was a boon to their spirits as well. Just the thought of the meal ahead was enough to get them laughing again. As special forces they were used to extraordinarily hard conditions, had to train through them, but at the end of the day they were still human. The relentless slogging dragged them down emotionally as well as physically.

Just the sight of the snake was enough to re-energize Aiden. They would make it out of this damn jungle alive and they would figure out how to make the Silverstone Collaborative pay for what they'd done. And maybe, *maybe*, he'd be able to connect with his brother.

The gnawing hunger in his gut got worse when the smell of the meat reached Aiden's nose. It was only knowing that if he ate it raw he'd be doubled over in the bush like Wulfe had been a few days ago. It took an agonizing twenty minutes to cook the meat fully, then Wulfe began tearing pieces off the stick and handing them out.

It melted like butter in Aiden's mouth. He'd had snake before, many times in fact, but for some reason this one tasted the best. Maybe it was because they were so hungry.

They ate well that night, and overall had a better outlook on their situation.

"I like dinner at your house, TJ," Aiden told him, grinning.

The younger man laughed and it was the most lighthearted Aiden had ever seen him.

CHAPTER SEVEN

I n the downtime from hiking, they developed exercises to work their minds. When they'd been in the camp, he'd noticed the 'static' from the people around him. As he talked to the other three they realized several things. They had to be closer to feel good emotions radiating off a person, usually within about ten feet. But if the person was having a bad day, it seemed to radiate out further. And whether they realized it or not as soon as they started the Ayahuasca serum their own moods began to deteriorate because they were picking up on the negative feelings of the techs and doctors around them that didn't like living in the camp.

They needed to find a way to block out all that miscellaneous noise.

Fontana had come up with the wall building exercise. Three of the men would focus on the fourth, barraging him with negative ideas and thoughts and feelings. He would have to imagine building a wall inside his mind to block all of that noise out. It was hard, and they realized they needed to start out one on one before adding the other two. So, they broke into teams and practiced barraging and shielding, then they would switch partners. Fontana was the best at barraging and Wulfe was the best at shielding. Watching the two of them go at each other was fascinating. From the outside Aiden saw two men sitting on the ground. Their fists were clenched and their bearded faces calm. But if you looked from the inside you could see how viciously they fought against one another.

Aiden much preferred to barrage than shield. It didn't seem to take as much energy to strike. Or maybe he was just better at it, like Fontana.

Even Wulfe had issues holding his shields when they all barraged him, though, and it was an exercise they needed to practice a lot.

They'd been in the jungle for two weeks when they hacked through the vegetation and onto a road. Aiden damn near fell on the blade he was so surprised. Looking one way, then the next, he stared until the other men joined him.

"Do we follow it?" TJ asked.

"It would make our lives a hell of a lot easier."

Fontana's leg was still giving him grief. It would definitely be easier for him to travel on the road, even as rough and rutted as it appeared.

"I don't believe this is a high traffic area," Wulfe said. "If we hear a vehicle coming we can dive into the brush."

They all agreed and headed east. They finally began to cover some serious ground. Aiden felt like they covered more that day than they had in five days blazing through the bush. Only once did they have to vacate the road, and that was to a man on a motorcycle. When they got back on the road they settled into an easy jog. In spite of the hunger constantly riding all of them, his bones settled into stride a lot easier than when they'd first escaped. Fontana maintained for at least two miles before he had to pull up to a walk.

That was worrying. For some reason this break wasn't healing as well as others they'd had. Aiden worried for his buddy, because that limp could threaten his life someday.

They walked into the night, resting only briefly to rehydrate and check the map. It looked like they were a few miles from a village called Muráta. There was no information about it, just the six letters of its name and where it was in relation to the coast. They were still such a long way from recovery, but he had hope. Now that they were near a road they would travel a lot faster than they had been, and if they could find a vehicle or someone to give them a ride they would be set.

Wulfe had suggested that his brother was probably the best option to call. Nikolas Terberger was a powerhouse who owned a major technology firm in Berlin and he would have both the savvy and money to get them out of the Amazon. They just had to make it to a place big enough to support a telephone and an airport. They had Dr. Shu's satellite phone, but they refused to use it until they were close to extraction. The Collaborative would figure out the phone's location as soon as it powered up.

So, they continued to walk. Aiden's white nurse shoes were damn near falling apart after hiking so far. Surprisingly, the sandals Fontana and Aiden had found were holding up well, better than Aiden would have ever expected.

Their clothes were ragged though, and they weren't much better. They'd eaten the last of the snake already and they needed to find something else to eat. Maybe, in the village, they could barter with the last few flashlights they had or something.

They started seeing signs of the village the next morning. A motorbike roared past them heading west. They hadn't even heard it before it came around a bend toward them. The man on the bike looked at them curiously but didn't stop.

Once he was passed, they all shared a glance. That man was a major security issue. They needed to be more careful.

Breaking into the brush they reconned the village, gauging size and how many people it held.

No more than about twenty families, and they seemed destitute. Aiden knew just by looking that they didn't have anything to spare, and there was a general feeling of hopelessness radiating from the area.

Should we even go in?

Aiden glanced at Wulfe, who shrugged his broad shoulders. *I don't think they're any better off than we are.*

They were just about to leave when they saw a white man walk into the village.

The man had to be part of a research team or something, because he had two porters carrying large steel boxes coming up the trail behind him. They'd crossed over that trail earlier and assumed it went to a field or stream, but they hadn't explored more than a few yards before circling on around the village.

The man looked around for something, but when he didn't see it he motioned to a shade tree, where the men dropped the four boxes and he sat on one. It was obvious he had been here before because no one raised a ruckus.

The four of them looked at each other, wondering whether they should approach the man or not.

TJ with the lame ass camper routine again? Fontana asked.

TJ rolled his eyes. *Thanks.*

The idea had merit, though, even he realized that. He resettled the bedraggled backpack over his shoulders, sighed, and headed through the brush.

The villagers seemed to be used to the man in the khaki shirt and hat but when TJ walked out of the jungle, voices raised in surprise. TJ waved weakly, and Aiden knew it was only partially a show. None of them were at peak perfor-mance right now thanks to lack of decent nutrition.

The man on the box stood up, looking tense, but TJ went to a couple of villagers, asking for help. One woman waved him toward the well in the middle of the village. She gave him a surprisingly sweet, gap-toothed smile, nodding that he was welcome to the water.

That was exceedingly generous, Aiden thought.

TJ moved to the well and hauled up the bucket tied to the rope. Then, very carefully, he filled the water bottles he had. Before he lowered the bucket he grabbed the cup off the peg at the side of the well and scooped out a cupful, drinking thirstily. Lowering the bucket back down into the water he returned to the woman and offered her a flashlight.

The woman took it with a giggle, pushing the power button on and off again much like the child from the first village. TJ grinned with her, asking her a few questions. She waved down the road shook her head a couple of times. TJ was getting ready to leave when they heard the roar of vehi-cles coming down the road.

They were all a little stunned. With the thickness of the vegetation sound didn't travel through it well, and with the bend right outside the village there'd been a pretty complete sound break.

What do I do guys?

Just stay where you are, Wulfe told him. *Stick to your story.*

Three vehicles pulled into the village. Two looked to be Brazilian Army jeeps, and the other appeared to be an aid worker's vehicle. It had canvas sides and seemed to be loaded with supplies. As soon as they parked, several unarmed men jumped down from the panel sided vehicle and started unloading boxes. The villagers cheered and started heading for the supplies.

At the same time, though, two of the soldiers spied TJ and started heading toward him, weapons up and ready. TJ held his hands up, showing them he was defenseless, and let them pat him down. He hadn't entered the village with any of the weapons the group had.

Aiden, watch TJ, Wulfe ordered. *I think they have something else going on here.*

The second Army jeep held the person in charge, because he walked across to the man that had been sitting on the boxes. Some tense words were exchanged and the white man shook his head, obviously trying to disavow knowledge of TJ. He motioned to the silver boxes and the Army commander moved over to them. Flipping the lid on one he drew out a long weapon.

Oh, shit. It's an arms deal. They're using the aid workers as cover.

TJ scowled, obviously hearing Fontana's words.

What do I do?

Finesse them, Fontana snapped.

TJ smiled at the two army men and said a few words, keeping a friendly expression on his face. The men looked at each other, then back at TJ. He said the same thing again and the men turned to walk away. TJ tried to turn casually to return to the bush, but the man in charge spotted him and screamed at his men. They snapped out of whatever TJ had told them to do and started after him.

TJ broke into a run, backpack thumping on his back as he got his feet moving. The villagers hadn't even noticed what was going on, they were so focused on receiving food, until the first weapon went off. Screaming, the villagers scattered. TJ took advantage of the pandemonium and plowed into the crowd.

Aiden was ready to run in if he needed support, but it looked like he was going to make it back. Then a fifth soldier they hadn't seen before circled the back of the aid truck. Taking aim with his sidearm, he fired. TJ went down like a ton of bricks. Aiden wasn't sure where he was hit, but he jumped out of the brush to go to his teammate. Wulfe was right beside him, weapon already firing. They took out the soldier at the rear of the truck, then the other two about to reach TJ. The commander in charge drew his own weapon but he was too far away to have any effect.

Fontana, the jeep!

Oh, God yes, transportation. If they were making this kind of ruckus they might as well go all the way and steal a jeep.

Wulfe circled the trucks and went toward the gun deal in progress. The man in khaki disappeared into the bush, following his porters, but the commander and his assistant still stood at the boxes, obviously reluctant to lose them. Wulfe took them down without hesitation.

The gunfire stopped. The aid workers and several villagers were huddled around the truck, a grim stoicism to their expressions. Gunfights happened and they knew enough not to choose sides. Aiden skidded to a stop beside TJ and rolled him over. There was blood on the guy's arm and a line on his temple, which was bleeding pretty well, but otherwise he looked intact. "Wake up, dude!"

TJ blinked his eyes open, looking a little dazed. "What happened?"

"You danced with bullets," Aiden grinned, brushing dirt off his face.

TJ sat up, then got to his feet, looking around. "Oh, hell, did we do that?"

"Yeah."

They jogged to the jeep Fontana was climbing into. "Aiden, take the second jeep."

Immediately understanding Fontana's plan, Aiden headed for the other jeep, veering into the bush to grab their packs. If they took both of the jeeps no one would be able to report them unless the aid worker's truck had a radio. Even if they did it wouldn't be Army quality. TJ hopped in beside him. Wulfe jumped into the front jeep with Fontana, and they tore out of there.

Aiden had known that the rutted road was treacherous. Hell, just walking on it had been hard enough. But in a jeep, going as fast as it could go, the road turned downright deadly. They went through several rutted streams, around downed logs and through overgrown patches. In the middle of their escape it started to pour the rain down, making the slogging even that much harder.

Barrage and shield!

With that one warning Fontana started beating at their minds. What the ever-loving fuck! Aiden felt his mind being struck and he had to focus like he never had before. Twice he almost veered into the brush from the strength of the attack, but after a while he figured out how to compartmentalize what he was doing. Then he turned the tables on Fontana and started mentally hammering on his shields. Aiden was gratified to see Fontana lose control as well before he got his vehicle in line.

After about an hour of hard driving and only passing one other vehicle, Fontana found them a place to hide within the trees.

"We're about to hit a larger village," Fontana told them when they jumped out. "We need to strip everything out of the second vehicle we need and just take one. We're more likely to blend in that way. TJ, you okay?"

The Ranger nodded. He'd wrapped his head to get it to stop bleeding, and managed to patch his own arm, all while going eighty miles an hour over rutted Amazon roads. "I'm like an old dog, I guess. I take a licking and keep on hunting."

Aiden laughed. "We're all old dogs."

"No," TJ corrected. "We're Dogs of War."

They all looked at each other. That had a decent ring to it, and it applied to them in several different connotations. They nodded. *Dogs of War*, they agreed.

CHAPTER EIGHT

They disabled the stripped-out jeep and left it in the jungle, then drove hell-for-leather to the east. At some point they had to reach civilization.

I think when we get to Belém on the coast, Fontana said, broadcasting to them all, *you can turn on that sat phone and contact your brother. Then we turn ghost until he can make arrangements for us.*

Agreed.

Fontana nodded once. It sounded easy enough but Aiden knew it wouldn't be.

They traveled for miles, until they ran out of gas. They refilled with the twelve gallon can on the back of the jeep, and he prayed that their destination would be within the next hundred and fifty miles or they'd be in trouble. Wulfe took over driving for a while, until the sun went down, then Aiden took over.

Driving in the barely lit dark through the Amazon was a bit of a trip. It felt like he was driving through a tunnel, the trees and bushes crowded around him so tight. It was so much better to drive at night, though. People couldn't see what you were in, and when you'd stolen a jeep from the Brazilian Army, that was priceless.

It gave him time to think about everything they'd done. He had no idea how many miles they'd traveled on foot, but it had to be a huge number. The orderly shoes were barely straps of fabric held together, and his clothes weren't much better. They'd used everything they had hard, including the urban outfitter's camping gear. He glanced in the rearview mirror. Fontana and Wulfe were barely awake in the back and they were all exhausted.

Houses started to pop up at the side of the road, and the road became smoother. Then they came to a crossroads, but Fontana waved him straight through. It was the first secondary road Aiden had seen.

He'd been driving an hour when he realized there was a bit of an orange glow to the east.

Think that's the city? he asked TJ.

The other man shrugged, not even wincing. The wound on his head was all but sealed, so Aiden assumed the one on his shoulder was as well.

The road started to become more crowded, then it dead-ended into a paved road. Following the glow, Aiden turned left, along with most of the rest of the traffic, and they crossed a huge bridge over murky brown water. There was a river to the left of them now as well.

"Fontana, get that map out and see where the airport is."

The other man did, and told him where to turn left, but Wulfe waved him on, into the heart of the city. Aiden wasn't prepared for the massive expanse of the city, and the amount of skyscrapers reaching for the sky. It was a tiny spot on the map, but he should have expected more. This was the port at the mouth of the Amazon and close to the Atlantic. From the looks of things they did brisk business in both river and ocean going cargo.

"Find busy shopping area, Will. We will leave jeep and call my brother."

Aiden nodded and continued to head toward the coast, assuming that there would be some type of busy commercial center. And he was right. Actually, they got into a touristy section and it just seemed to go on and on.

"Stop! Pull in there."

Wulfe pointed into a busy parking garage next to a massive shopping mall. They took the ticket the machine spit out and left it on the dash for the Brazilian Army to take care of. Aiden wound his way up through the floors of cars to the least crowded floor, parked in the far corner and they got out.

"We should go through the packs and at least try to clean up," Aiden said. "There are plenty of people here, but we need to not draw attention to ourselves."

They all agreed and started pawing through their things. Aiden decided that the black outfit he was wearing was the best he had, in spite of the dirt. The shoes would just have to stand out, until he could get something else. If he'd been smart he could have taken the boots from the dead men when they stole the jeeps but they had been kinda rushed. As it was, he'd have to wear the damn nurse shoes, which weren't even slightly decent. Aiden doused one of the t-shirts with water, then used it to scrub his face and over his head. Their hair was growing back in, but it would take a while.

By the time they were done they were as clean as they could make themselves, which wasn't very. It had been weeks since they'd had any type of shower other than a waterfall, and even longer than that since they'd used any kind of soap. They all had a manly funk to them that they'd gotten used to but would probably get them banned from any public places. Normally he'd have been embarrassed as hell to even think about walking out into public, but he was too desperate to get out of the country to care.

Once they were clean they started going through the rest of the equipment they had and consolidating the packs. The rifles wouldn't do them any good anymore, so they disabled them and piled them in the back seat. They did take all the handguns, as well as the shells for them. Once they were ready, Aiden handed Wulfe the plastic bag with Dr. Shu's satellite phone and battery in it.

Anxiety surged in his gut. What if he didn't get through to him? Did they have a backup number to call?

Putting the pieces of the phone together Wulfe punched in a telephone number from memory. They all waited in silence, listening to the sound of the phone ringing on the other end. Finally, a man answered, sounded aggravated and pissed off.

Wulfe was the stalwart one of the group, but when he heard the sound of his brother's voice, his eyes teared up. He turned away from the men and they allowed him that peace. If they'd been in the same position they would want privacy as well.

Aiden knew enough German to understand that Wulfe was giving Nikolas a truncated version of events. He reported to his brother where they were and what they needed, and Nikolas didn't hesitate. Wulfe kept the call under a minute long, but Aiden knew that they had just put a target on their backs.

"It will take him twelve hours to get plane here. He was in Miami on business and is refueling now. We have to stay out of sight until then. We have money coming to the Western Union across the street. It was why I had you pull in," he grinned.

Wulfe was happy to finally talk to his brother, it was there in his expression and voice. He'd spoken about the man as if he walked on water. If Nikolas could get them money and out of the country within a day, Aiden would be forced to believe it as well.

The phone beeped in Wulfe's hand and he looked at the screen. A message had come in dated two weeks ago, about a week after they'd broken out of the camp. *I don't know who you are yet, but I'm going to kill you.*

They all saw the message, and knew exactly who it was from. Wulfe powered down the phone and removed the battery, then wrapped the two pieces in the plastic bag it had been in for the trek through the jungle.

With a final shared look they headed down the stairs. Being in the city like this would test the shielding they'd been practicing, but it had to be done. The jeep was no longer an option. Aiden didn't know how long it would take for the Collaborative to find them after the phone call, but he had a feeling it wouldn't be long. Fontana left the keys to the jeep on the front seat, if some enterprising thief did them a solid and kept it out of the army's hands for a bit longer, that was all to the good.

Wulfe headed into the Western Union to retrieve the money his brother sent, with TJ acting as interpreter. Fontana and Aiden stood outside the little grocery, trying to look less conspicuous than they felt. Wulfe returned with several bottles of water, handing them out, and several packaged sandwiches.

Aiden didn't even remember what was on the bread, but he ate it, then wished he had four more. The others ate their food just as fast, then looked around, trying to decide where to go. He felt like a rat in a maze and he wanted out of it.

Nikolas wants us to meet him at a small airport on the east side, not the main airport. As long as we're there within about ten hours, we should be good. I suggest we find some hot food as well as a way to clean up.

Sounds good to me, Fontana agreed.

They headed down the street, looking for a street food vendor. Wulfe handed each of them a wad of money and Aiden stared at it. It had been so long since he'd even seen any kind of money much less held it in his hand that it felt strange.

They wandered down an alley and when they came out, they were in the middle of a bustling street market. It was after eight in the evening, but that apparently didn't matter to the Brazilians. When he heard the live music playing, he understood. There were a lot of people here and if they'd come for the music there was a very good chance they would shop as well.

Aiden stopped at the first street food vendor he saw. A man sold skewers of meat. Aiden held up two fingers and the man started getting the food from the grill.

Even after he paid and took a bite, Aiden had no idea what he was eating and he didn't care. It was damn good, he knew that, and he almost went back for a second helping, but there were other food stalls.

They ate their way through the market, picking up clothing items here and there. They all found decent boots or shoes to wear and just having something on their feet that was so solid a feeling they had to pause to look at each other in satisfaction. Fontana handed them ball caps and sunglasses for the next day.

With the crush of people around them Aiden worried they would have to shield like crazy, but the entire crowd was projecting a good mood vibe. They picked up a few grumblings from individuals, but nothing so strong that they couldn't control it.

And whether they realized it or not, the four of them settled into a classic fire team wedge formation. Fontana took point, then came Wulfe and Rector, and Aiden brought up the rear. They moved through the crowds like they'd done it many times before.

Watch the drunk on the left.

Badges to our six.

Aiden couldn't believe how much he'd come to admire these men. They'd each given their all in every part of their escape. *You guys are awesome*, he thought to them.

Fontana reached out and gripped his shoulder. *You're not so bad yourself, Will. Thank you for digging in my ass.*

Aiden choked out a laugh. *It was one of the highlights of my life.*

They ate enough food for an entire platoon of men, then paused to listen to the live band. It was surreal to be here, knowing that less than five hundred miles away there was a camp where men were being tortured. They stopped at a magazine stand and looked at the pictures. TJ read them some of the highlights. Who'd have thought that a being gone from their world for nearly a year could change so much.

What day is it? Anyone know?

They all shrugged and he guessed it didn't really matter. As long as they were together and safe.

For hours they moved through the streets like they had a purpose, moving away from the location where Wulfe had made the call on the sat phone. The further they were away from that mess the better. If they could hang out somewhere for the night, in the morning they could get a taxi to the airport. After a while they found a riverfront park and they looked out over the mighty, muddy Amazon. It was like looking out onto the ocean. They couldn't see the far side bank, only lights from the ships. Even this late at night the ship traffic seemed busy. In between the heavy carrier ships were smaller fishing vessels. It was a beautiful sight.

When they came to a small stretch of beach, they settled onto their asses to watch some night trawling. Fontana stretched out his leg in front of him and Aiden knew it was hurting him, but he hadn't complained a bit. He'd moved like it hadn't bothered him at all, until now.

"What are we going to do after your brother gets here?"

Wulfe shrugged, arms propped on his knees as he looked out over the water. "Not sure."

"We have to tell someone," TJ said.

"But who?"

They all knew that their governments were complicit with what had gone on. Aiden would like to think that the United States thought more of their military, but there were enough shady characters in Washington that they might have slipped something through without outright saying what the exercise was. At least, that's what he hoped. It would be seriously fucked up if a group of his commanders got together and decided to just hand him over to *that*.

"I think we need to explore the information we've stolen and investigate," Fontana said. "We can't go public outright because right now it's our word against the Collaborative's. They have such a sterling reputation that I don't think anyone would believe us."

"I don't think so either," TJ agreed. "They've damn near cured cancer. I can see them spinning it around to where they get support for using us like they did."

"We did, after all, agree to take part in the experiment," Fontana reminded them.

And didn't that burn all of their asses.

"But the conditions changed," Aiden argued. "They voided the agreement when they made us prisoners."

"We need to go underground for a while," Wulfe told them. "Investigate. Find out what is on the drives. Study the journal. Get our health back."

The thought of eating normally and sleeping normally seemed like a dream.

"If we stay under radar, use cash, stay mobile, they won't find us."

Wulfe seemed sure of his words but Aiden just wasn't. Imagining staying that far underground gave him a headache. They would have no life. "How do we survive?"

Wulfe waved a hand in the night. "Family has money. It is not a consideration."

Aiden eyed Wulfe. "If you're so rich why were you in the military?"

"Tradition," he said simply.

Ah, yes. Then there was that. Family tradition.

"It might take them a while to figure out who we are, and then they will know who our families are," Aiden reminded them.

The techs had used computers to log in the info about the experiments, and Shu had regularly carried around a tablet, but Aiden didn't think they had the ability to upload to the company regularly. There had been no cell service, he knew that for sure, but he wasn't sure if the Collaborative had satellite coverage over the area. Surely they had the initial information about the subjects, and the background investigation information, but he didn't know how often that info had been updated. It would take them a while to cross-reference the information they had with the subjects left in the camp.

"Then we make sure our families are secure," TJ said.

There was so much to think about and do, but they were tired. They'd been up before dawn and a lot had happened since then. Almost as one they shimmied down into the sand of the beach. *We'll think more tomorrow, Americans.*

CHAPTER NINE

They woke to waves lapping at their stretched out feet and a man in a blue uniform standing over top of them. Aiden bolted into a sitting position. "TJ," he hissed.

The other man rolled over, glancing blearily at the morning, then he saw the cop and went still. The blue-uniformed cop spewed something at them angrily and TJ stood, brushing the seat of his pants off.

Get up! He's just moving us on.

The other three scrambled to their feet, nodding as if they understood what he was yelling at them. Grabbing the bags they hurried off the beach, aware that the cop stood behind them watching.

That was too close.

They started walking, trying to blend in with the crowds. They had another four hours before they could expect to see Wulfe's brother. Getting to the airport would take them less than twenty minutes. They could probably walk to it.

I think we should get a burner phone, or four. Just in case.

Wulfe nodded. *Probably smart.*

First, though, was food. After walking a few blocks, they found a popular chain restaurant, known the world over.

Oh, fuck me... I think I've died and gone to heaven, Fontana moaned. *I want two of everything.*

They walked out of the restaurant with three large bags of food and two trays of drinks, and found an out of the way spot outside to sit and eat. Aiden could have wept from the taste of the bacon and the biscuit. And cheese! He hadn't had cheese in so long...

They ate almost all the food and drank all of the four large orange juices and four coffees.

"I think I'm going to be sick, y'all," TJ sighed. "I need another nap."

They all did, but it wasn't going to happen. Instead, they started walking. When they came upon another corner market they ducked in to check it out. It was surprisingly well-stocked. Aiden picked out four cell phone kits and added minute cards.

It took them a bit to set up the phones but when they were done they all felt more secure about having a way to contact someone, most importantly each other.

It was strange looking at the device because he used to be a bit of a tech guy himself, with the latest phones and gadgets. He didn't even recognize this brand, though, or any of the logos on the home screen. Between the phone and the newspaper articles, he felt very disconnected.

They swapped numbers and pocketed the devices. Then they walked for another hour.

When it was close enough to the time, they headed toward the small, private airfield Nikolas had directed them to. It wasn't especially far from the international airport and hopefully, if by chance the Bitch in Blue managed to track them down from the sat phone call, she would be looking there. Or at one of the shipping ports. The tiny little private landing strip might not even catch her notice.

Wulfe stopped beneath a broad palmed shade tree and pulled out the burner phone. Punching in his brother's number he sent off a text.

Almost immediately he received a response. Aiden peered over his shoulder.

On the tarmac fueling up. Go to delivery gate on south side of airport. Security is waiting for you. Tell them you are my passengers. They have been paid.

The south side was ahead of them and to the right. They started walking, constantly scanning the area around them. They were off the main tourist areas so seeing four grown men walking together was a bit strange, but they kept going. Aiden felt like he was under a sniper's scope. The hairs on the back of his neck lifted. The feeling got so bad that he had to stop. He stepped into the shade at the side of the street.

Hang on a sec, guys.

They stilled immediately, and he appreciated that.

Something doesn't feel right.

The men looked around, trying to see what Aiden was feeling, but none of them saw anything.

What is it? Fontana asked.

I'm not sure but the last time I felt this you ended up with a machete in your ass.

In the bright light of day Fontana actually paled. It would have been funny if they weren't in their current situation.

Aiden opened his senses, trying to understand what he was feeling. There weren't a lot of people around, certainly no one associated with the Collaborative, he didn't think. The day was fairly sleepy. Then he spotted it. Something about the black SUV struck him as wrong, and he didn't know why. But as soon as he focused in on the people inside the vehicle, he understood. There was vigilance and determination from one side of the car, and somnolent antipathy on the other side. The two people inside the vehicle couldn't be more different.

It was the determined one that worried him.

Black SUV at ten o'clock.

They all looked in that direction. *Man, that dude is pissed*, Fontana said eventually. *What's his deal?*

Not sure, but we either need to backtrack and come in from the east or distract them.

How the fuck do we do that? Rector asked.

Aiden wasn't exactly sure. *We could force them to act upon us.*

Fontana rubbed a hand over his neck. *If we get close enough to the vehicle we can make him do something, but it may not be a good idea to draw attention in the middle of the day.*

Agreed.

I say we circle around, TJ said.

In the end it didn't matter, because they were spotted. Not by the guys in the car but by the SUV that pulled up behind them.

"Stop right there," a voice called out.

All four of them went still. Not Brazilian police or Army, they'd be speaking Portuguese. Aiden's gut clenched and fear ran through his veins. He hated being snuck up upon.

"Turn around."

All four turned around. There was a fairly young man standing on the far side of the vehicle in the V from the open door. He pointed his weapon at the four of them, across the vehicle.

Aiden glanced to the right. The two men slid out of the other vehicle and the one that he'd felt the aggression from, a heavier-set balding man, seemed royally pissed. His aggression spiked and he drew his weapon, holding it at his side.

Looking at the younger man, understanding he would have to die, Aiden told him, "They're coming to kill you."

The young man glanced at the two stalking down the street. They were actually headed toward Aiden's group but there was enough doubt there that the young man felt insecure. He pivoted, aiming his weapon at the main guard. "Stop right there. I have this under control."

They're going to shoot you, Aiden told him, pushing. *Defend yourself.*

The young guard fired his weapon. Repeatedly.

He hit his target. The older man staggered, spinning to the ground. But the aggressive guy's sleepy companion suddenly woke up. He fired at the SUV and the young man, and Aiden knew as soon as the bullet tore through the door that the kid was dead. He went down firing, though. By the time it was all said and done, all three of the guards were dead.

Let's take this as the gift it was meant to be and get the fuck out of here.

Conscious that there might be witnesses, they turned and walked away as casually as possible. They were at the security gate within minutes and the man waved them through, over the protests of his partner.

He spouted a bunch of Portuguese and TJ nodded, giving him a wave.

Hangar twelve. Three buildings down.

They turned and walked. Aiden felt even more exposed now that they were in such an open area. There were no trees or buildings or cars to take cover behind. They hurried, passing one hangar, then two. The third hangar stood wide open, occupied by a sleek, black private jet. A man in a black suit waited on the stairs and waved.

For the first time in weeks he felt hope that they were actually going to get out of this shithole situation.

Wulfe broke into a jog and the men followed along behind. Nikolas Terberger looked so similar to his brother, there was no doubt about who stood waiting for them. Tears glittered in his eyes as he dragged Wulfe into a back-slapping hug, and Wulfe pulled him tight. Then he leaned back enough to cup his hands around Nik's neck, talking to him softly. They nodded together, smiling and laughing.

It made Aiden think of his own brother. If the guy was still out there he wanted to know him someday. He couldn't imagine being greeted like Wulfe just was, but it might be worth checking out the possibility.

"We are ready to go," Nik told them, shaking each man's hand as they climbed the stairs. "Take a seat and I'll let the pilot know."

There were two attendants, one male and one female. They took the men's bedraggled bags and guided them to plush leather seats. Then they began handing out refreshments. Aiden sank into the leather and let out a groan. Comfort. It was the most amazing feeling. Then embarrassment washed over him. He was so rank. In spite of that, though, he took the beer the attendant handed him and took a long swallow. *Oh, fuck yeah…*

As soon as the door closed behind them the plane engines began to whine with power. They pulled out of the hangar and rumbled down the long taxiway. They made the turn, paused, and the engines whined to full pitch. The brakes released, and they launched down the runway, the landscape speeding by. As the wheels left the tarmac, he looked out the window at the hangar they'd just left.

A black SUV was parked in front of it and Priscilla Mattingly stood on the tarmac, hands on her hips as she watched them take off. Knowing he was too far away, he flipped her the bird anyway.

She could roast in hell.

———

On the trip back to Miami, Nik let them use his private bathroom in the back of the plane. For the first time in almost a year, Aiden stood beneath the *hot* water of a shower, in complete privacy, and let some of his emotions go. It had been so long since he'd felt like a human being rather than a prisoner or a damn lab rat. His abused muscles relaxed and if he'd had room he probably would have slumped to the floor to enjoy it.

They had so much to do. He had a feeling that breaking out of the camp and forging through the jungle had been the easiest leg of this journey they were on.

He didn't know how they were going to proceed, but right this minute they had leverage. And backing, if Wulfe was to be believed. They needed to recover and get their ducks in order, then try to investigate who in their governments had handed them over to the Silverstone Collaborative.

Then the Dogs of War would be coming for them.

All of them.

To Be Continued...

If you would like to read Chapter One of Chaos, read ahead!

ALSO BY J.M. MADDEN

If you would like to read about the 'combat modified' veterans of the
Lost and Found Investigative Service, check out these books
on her website, JMMadden.com :

The Embattled Road (FREE prequel)

Duncan, John and Chad

Embattled Hearts-Book 1 (FREE)

John and Shannon

Embattled Minds-Book 2

Zeke and Ember

Embattled Home-Book 3

Chad and Lora

Embattled SEAL- Book 4

Harper and Cat

Embattled Ever After- Book 5

Duncan and Alex

Her Forever Hero- Grif

Grif and Kendall

Second Time Around

A Needful Heart

Wet Dream

Love on the Line

The Billionaire's Secret Obsession

The Awakening Society- FREE

Tempt Me

If you'd like to connect with me on social media and keep updated on my releases, try these links:

Jmmadden.com/newsletter

JMMadden.com

Authorjmmadden

@authorjmmadden

And of course you can always email me at authorjmmadden@gmail.com

ABOUT THE AUTHOR

NY Times and USA Today Bestselling author J.M. Madden writes compelling romances between 'combat modified' military men and the women who love them. J.M. Madden loves any and all good love stories, most particularly her own. She has two beautiful children and a husband who always keeps her on her toes.

J.M. was a Deputy Sheriff in Ohio for nine years, until hubby moved the clan to Kentucky. When not chasing the family around, she's at the computer, reading and writing, perfecting her craft. She occasionally takes breaks to feed her animal horde and is trying to control her office-supply addiction, but both tasks are uphill battles. Happily, she is writing full-time and always has several projects in the works. She also dearly loves to hear from readers! So, drop her a line. She'll respond.

AFTERWORD

If you would like to read book 1 of the Dogs Of War series go to **my website** for all the current links!

And Now... a taste of Chaos, Book 1 in the Dogs of War.... Available Now!

"Can I help you?"

Aiden froze at the sound of the smoky, bluesy woman's voice, unwilling to turn around. There were only three times he'd ever been snuck up upon, this being the third, and he was shocked. Had his skills degraded that much? Fuck...

Slowly, he turned. A staggeringly beautiful woman stood less than twenty feet behind him, well within killing distance. The afternoon sunlight shone on her bright strawberry-blond ponytail, a light breeze playing with the bangs hanging over her forehead. The look on her heart-shaped face suggested she'd just stumbled across something interesting. She had one lean hip cocked, but something about the way she stood told him she was more than she appeared. He could have been dead.

What a great way to die, at the hands of such a beautiful

woman.

One hand tugged open the side of her jacket, enough for him to see the badge. "I asked you a question. Is there something you're looking for here?"

Her unflinching, blue-gray eyes narrowed, waiting for a response.

Cop. Figured. Only seeing too many things put that kind of experience on a face. He was sure his looked the same. Actually, his face looked worse, surely.

She shifted her stance and Aiden realized he had tightened his own, as if readying for a fight. Deliberately, he took a relaxing breath and shoved his hands into his pockets.

Within a split second, the flame-haired woman drew down on him with a steadiness and speed that spoke of true familiarity with her weapon. "Hold it right there," she ordered, her voice losing that sexy edge.

Aiden had fired enough Sig Sauers to know that the weapon she held in her hand would more than injure him. If she targeted correctly she could kill him with one shot. Maybe.

Taking cautious steps, she advanced on him. "You need to remove your hands from your pockets. Left first."

Aiden eased his hand out and up, pissed at the ridiculous situation. And his own stupidity.

"Now, right."

He did as he was told until he stood with his hands in the air. "I should not have moved. That was my mistake."

"Yes, it was. Interlace your fingers behind your head."

Aiden stilled at her steady words. He would allow her to pat him down if she felt she needed to but he would not allow her to handcuff him. "I'm not carrying anything," he told her steadily. And for the first time in a long time it was true. Guilt had been riding him and he hadn't been thinking clearly when he'd headed here.

"Can't take your word for that, sorry."

"You should take my word for it though," he told her clearly. "I'm safe to you. I promise."

He didn't *finesse* her, although he did put enough suggestion into the words that she should have been mollified, but she completely ignored what he said and moved in behind him.

A firm touch patted its way down his body, from collar to waist to ankles, leaving no area untouched. He felt the warmth of her body shift behind him as she moved lower, patting down his pant legs. At any point, Aiden could have taken her down with ease, with a single thought, but he allowed her to confirm her safety. And she did it with a commendable thoroughness. Maybe it wouldn't have been so easy to take her down...The woman stepped back.

And he missed the feel of her touch.

"You may lower your hands but no sudden movements."

Dropping his hands to his side, he waited for her next order.

"Turn around. And tell me what the hell you're doing here."

She had re-holstered her weapon, but her hand rested on the butt of the gun, ready. Aiden clenched his jaw, hating the need to lie his ass off. Again. He could give her a partial truth at least. "I was looking for someone. A homeless guy that used to hang around out here. Somebody said something bad had happened and I just wanted to check on him."

She cocked her head, her blue eyes narrowing in consideration. "What's the homeless guy's name?"

Aiden didn't hesitate. "Roman. Older guy, gray beard, usually has a gray hat on. Used to be a librarian."

The woman continued to stare at him and Aiden actually shifted in discomfort, before he forced his body to stillness.

Roman was a real guy, he just hadn't hung around in this area for months.

But did she know that?

———

The guy was full of shit.

Angela Holloway narrowed her eyes and cocked her head, debating whether or not she could take the man in for questioning. Technically, he hadn't done anything wrong. He was just acting weird, hunkered down and looking at exactly where all the blood had been. As if he had known where the puddle had been. When he'd first turned around there had been desolate sorrow in his chocolate brown eyes.

She'd thought he was one of the homeless, with his dingy black sweatshirt and ball cap, but now she wasn't sure. His deep-set eyes were clear, and he didn't appear to be under the influence of alcohol or drugs. But he definitely seemed to want to fly under the radar. His clothes were nondescript enough to fit in almost anywhere, especially in Colorado, known for its rugged nature and even more rugged people. He seemed to be decently good-looking, even though he'd tried to hide most of his face with a thick dark beard. Longish nut-brown hair hung over his shoulders. Honestly, he looked like every other Hipster she dealt with every day. The only reason he'd drawn her attention was because of *where* he was.

She actually knew the Roman this guy was talking about. An old Vietnam vet who'd been on the streets for at least nine or ten years. As long as she'd been a cop. But he didn't hang out in this neighborhood and he hadn't for the better part of a year.

"Roman stays closer to downtown these days, closer to the Mission so he can get out of the chilly nights."

She watched the skin around his eyes tighten and his gaze flick away. He didn't like that she'd called him on his information.

"Ah, okay. I'll go check around there then. Thank you."

She stopped his movement with a halting motion. "I'm not quite ready to let you go yet. Do you have ID on you?"

The dark bearded jaw tightened, and he sighed. "I don't, actually. I didn't expect to need it."

She frowned. "Did you drive here?"

"No."

"Why don't you have identification on you?"

The man glowered, dark brows lowered over his dark eyes. Then, abruptly, his expression changed, and he gave her a sardonic smile.

Angela registered the change and sighed inside. Damn. He was going to try to flirt? Really?

For some reason, men always thought they were cuter than they actually were. Time after time she'd had suspects wiggle their brows or roll their hips toward her. When she'd been a uniformed street cop, they'd come at her, hands held out in front of them begging to be handcuffed. Sometimes she'd taken them up on their offer, depending upon how much of a nuisance they became. It had been a running joke in the squad-room. Send in the sweet-faced rookie and she'd haul their asses in. Angela was actually very proud of her arrest record.

This one actually was kinda cute, though, if a little rumpled. His clothes were dumpy and nondescript, his boots well worn. He had that bored, I-don't-really-care-what-you-think air, but his voice was really something. Soft and a little seductive, his words enunciated perfectly. If she'd been in a bar, she probably wouldn't have turned down a drink from him. She might even have let him steal a kiss. She didn't mind beards, especially when they come with that kind of voice.

"I just wasn't even thinking about my ID when I walked here. I only ever carry cash in my pockets."

Pulling a pad and pen from her jacket pocket, she lifted a brow at him. "Name, please?"

The easy going light left his eyes and his chin tipped up. Angela had seen the obstinate look before on other suspects. "If you don't tell me your name and social security number, I have to haul your ass downtown. Do you understand what I'm telling you?"

He shook his head. "I can't tell you that. I'm sorry."

Without hesitation, she started to move in on him. "Face the wall and put your hands behind your back."

He turned and faced the wall, but it seemed too easy. Angela dropped her notepad and pen to the ground and reached for the cuff-case at the base of her spine. Before she could even swing them around, the man had turned and wrapped his arms around her. She opened her mouth to yell, but his mouth settled on hers.

Shock rendered her mute. But the anger quickly began to move in.

Until his lips started to move on hers, and the beard began to tickle.

Chills shuddered down her spine as the man tightened his arms around her, snugging his hips into hers. She knew she needed to pull away but something besides his arms held her immobile. As his lips moved, she was struck with a sense of familiarity. No, she didn't know him, but it seemed deeper than that. Like her body recognized his.

Angela strained against his hold, but he deepened the kiss and she forgot what she'd been doing. The man tasted like sex. Raunchy, pounding, messy sex. And peppermint toothpaste. In spite of what her brain was telling her, her body began to respond.

And so did his. If she had been the only one affected by

what he was doing, she would have noticed that. But he was absolutely interested.

Turning her, he urged her back against the wall, pressing her hips with his own. Angela gasped at the feel of the hard ridge pressing against her. Somewhat instinctively she pushed back.

The man inhaled sharply, and the restraint was suddenly gone from her arms. His broad hands cupped her face, angling her jaw as his mouth moved. The tip of his tongue teased at the seam of her lips and she opened to taste him.

A rush of arousal hit her square between the eyes. Her nipples went hard against his broad chest and things lower in her body tightened, then loosened. His hands glided down her body, cupping her hips.

She heard the snick of handcuffs and a chill ran through her. When the man pulled away, there seemed to be genuine regret in his dark brown eyes. "I'm sorry I had to do this," he told her, clearing his voice. He backed away, hands held out.

Angela felt tightness on her waist and she jerked. What the hell had he done?

"You, you," she sputtered, totally, immediately pissed.

He winced and stared at her for a long moment, like he was waffling in his decision, then his eyes cooled and he turned away. As he disappeared around the corner of the building, Angela reached behind her to feel what was holding her. The man had handcuffed the belt loop of her jeans to a utility pole running horizontal across the building.

With a cry of outrage she dug in her pocket for the knife she always carried. It took her a minute to cut through the heavy fabric of the belt loop, but she did. As soon as she was able she bolted after the suspect, but he was gone.

Chaos is available on preorder and will be released June 26th!

Made in the USA
Columbia, SC
08 August 2018